T0329285

Boundaries

Emmanuel Fru Doh

Langaa Research & Publishing CIG
Mankon, Bamenda

Publisher
Langaa RPCIG
Langaa Research & Publishing Common Initiative Group
P.O. Box 902 Mankon
Bamenda
North West Region
Cameroon
Langaagrp@gmail.com
www.langaa-rpcig.net

Distributed in and outside N. America by African Books Collective
orders@africanbookscollective.com
www.africanbookscollective.com

ISBN: 9956-762-66-0

DISCLAIMER
All views expressed in this publication are those of the author and do
not necessarily reflect the views of Langaa RPCIG.

Dedication

To my dear friend Robson Sama,
To the memory of our mutual friend
Pong George Pong

&

To the Anglophone cause in Cameroon:
we must stand together and make our point
or let belly-politicians divide and maintain
us as national bastards in our fatherland.

To God Almighty be Praise and Glory

Chapter 1

The fervent and devoted catechist, Ndzem, looked up at the revealing face of the sky above the Bamenda Station hill as he walked down to the doctrine class from the Reverend Father's house where Father Alphonsus Freegan had summoned and reminded him of the upcoming First Holy Communion ceremony. Father Alphonsus, as the Christians fondly referred to him, was a burly looking man who virtually towered above every other person in the parish. His stern look, from a distance, immediately melted into a refreshingly friendly smile whenever anyone approached him, especially the kids. The children loved the gap he had between his upper incisors through which he had formed a habit of spraying spittle out of his mouth, unlike others who just spat "twah!" by the side. The children had to be ready for their First Holy Communion Examination within the next two weeks. This was the group, which, if successful, would receive First Holy Communion on Big-Day Maria, the feast of the Assumption of the Blessed Virgin Mary into heaven.

As usual, the examination held in Father's huge office with the new converts sitting round in a circle of which Father Alphonsus, sitting at his desk, was a part. He would go from pupil to pupil, beginning from his left, asking each to recite one prayer or the other that the catechumens should have memorized, along with questions about the doctrine of the Roman Catholic faith. In the process, he wrote down brief notes on how each pupil performed, and, in the end, the results were made known to the children. Those who passed, by answering the questions correctly and repeating the prayers well, were then to prepare for their First Holy

1

Communion: girls needed a white gown and pair of shoes and boys a white shirt and a white pair of shorts or trousers, depending on what the family could afford, and a pair of shoes also. Meanwhile, the catechist would spend the week before the ceremony showing the candidates how they would be seated in church on this great occasion, how they would process to the altar at communion time, and how to receive and consume the body of our Lord with reverence. They were, above all, to ensure it did not touch their teeth for fear it would bleed. If it was stuck to the roof of their mouths, they were to use only their tongue, never their fingers, to get it off. They were to keep sucking at it, without chewing, until it dissolved in their mouths and then they could swallow it. The catechist was thorough about this, as gently spoken as he was. He was a skinny man of average height, dark in complexion and sickly in gait, with smoke-stained lips and knuckles; he walked slowly and with an air of one in a daze. Father Alphonsus was urging the catechist who taught these classes every day, except on Saturdays, Sundays, and special feast days when there was no class, to ensure the catechumens were ready for the up-coming test.

"Ndzem, you hear me?"
"Yes, Father."
"Pikin dem must ready for exam. Okay?"
"Dem go ready, Father, and dem di do well."
"Good, good! Okay, go finish class then."
"Okay, Father," Ndzem answered, turned and walked out of the Father's office.

Ndzem, with a tired, worn out look on his face that his receding hairline did not help, was still in his late fifties only.

With his chin steeped in a mixture of grey and black hair that formed a thick long beard that practically rested on his chest each time he lowered his head, Ndzem could be mistaken for an ascetic of some sort. He was normally slow in the way he walked, with a preoccupied look always on his face. Notwithstanding, he always had a kind word and a welcoming smile for everyone who came his way. He was at his best though whenever he spoke the word of the Lord as he simply came alive.

It was already getting dark, so Ndzem marvelled as he looked up at the sky, and then it occurred to him that it was that time of the year again when places got dark a lot earlier than usual, such that one thought it was already midnight when it was just about 6:00pm. As he got closer to the classroom where the doctrine classes held, Ndzem could hear the children still repeating the lines he had instructed them to keep repeating when he answered the call to the Father's office. It was Pa Cook, as everyone in the mission called him by his job as Father Alphonsus' cook, who had come all the way down to call for him. The children were still chanting:

"Na who make you?"
"Na God make me."
"Why God make you?"
"God make me for sabi yi, for like yi, and for work for yi."

Ndzem had split the class of twenty-eight catechumens into two groups: one half asking the questions and the other answering in return.

"Okay, my children," Ndzem called out as he walked into the room, "I'm glad you're learning well, but it's time to go home, and remember that your doctrine exam comes up in two weeks. Tell your parents—two weeks!"

"Two weeks," the children repeated after him with emphasis.

Together they said the closing prayers with Ndzem leading, and then the children stormed out of the room running in every direction, shouting and calling out goodbyes to their friends; it was the end of one more doctrine class, which went on from 4:30pm to 6:00pm. As Ndzem walked back home, he thought of the thousands of children he had prepared for communion all through his career with an air of humble satisfaction, but his mind was heavy; it occurred to him the Lord did not seem to be keeping His own part of the bargain. It is His promise that the house of the honest man will want for nothing, yet his children did not seem to be thriving, especially his first son, his cane in old age as the people of the Grassfields hold it. It was as if whatever Musang set himself to do, he just could not bring it to fruition. Ndzem wondered how the Lord could pay him back in such coins. Nevertheless, he remained convinced that God's words could never go in vain, and so he kept trusting. "God works in strange ways," was his favourite slogan.

Pa Catechist, as everyone throughout Big Mankon referred to Ndzem, was one of the first catechists of St. Anselm's Parish, Big Mankon, a neighbourhood of Mankon town perched on a knoll next to the imposing Station hill, which lodges the government residential area and some offices. This was the main parish, with other satellite parishes in surrounding neighbourhoods like Bayele in Nkwen, Small Mankon in Azire, and Ntambeng Parishes. These, altogether, formed the heart of the Catholic Church in the burgeoning Bamenda metropolis. Pa Catechist was so devoted a Catholic

4

such that he gave up his richly paying business as an intermediary between coffee farmers and the Oversea Coffee Exporting Corporation (OCEC) to become a catechist. When at the very beginning the church spoke of the need for catechists and the reward awaiting them in heaven, Ndzem signed up to be trained. After completing his training to become a catechist, he did not hesitate returning two of his three wives back to their parents when the Church preached against polygamy and warned polygamists that they were continuing the tradition at the risk of losing their souls after death. He built a house for each wife back at her father's compound and left each well off with a little money and a field farmed and planted with different food crops before walking away. He stayed with his first wife, Mojoko, a woman from the coast.

When he walked back home from doctrine classes this evening, Ndzem joined Mojoko in the kitchen where they sat basking and sharing stories by the hearth as they roasted fresh corn for after dinner snacks. This was their way of being intimate, especially when the children were not around. This time, however, their concern was their first son, Musang, and his future. Unlike other children in the neighbourhood, they had never heard him talk seriously about what he would like to become as an adult. In the same manner, they had never seen a single girl come around to visit with him as they had established with other boys whose friends at school or former schoolmates stopped by from time to time for a visit. They could not help wondering if their son was all right, or if he was someone who could not interact with the opposite sex. After all, were it not for this new system of education they must submit to these days, which keeps them roaming from one school to another in pursuit of all kinds of certificates,

Musang should have been thinking of marriage already. Ndzem and Mojoko's love for their children was taking quite a toll on them because of how much they worried about their every move and predicament. As a result, they spent a lot of time praying and hoping their children would turn out good and successful in life. Musang, their oldest child, was a whole head taller than his father and fairer in complexion, the latter being a quality they said came from his mother's family but with the good looks his father has always had even from his days as a young man. It was not surprising then that each time Mojoko and her husband teased each other, Mojoko joked about her powerful genes, which passed on her complexion to her son. Ndzem, on the other hand, boasted about his looks, which he passed on to their son. He always ended up, as they laughed and enjoyed themselves, blaming Mojoko for having stressed him out so much that he looked nothing like he was when Mojoko fell for him. It was the consensus that Musang looked very much like his father, even Mojoko agreed to it. Even then, although girls found Musang attractive, he kept his distance and did not give them priority in his life, some obvious attention even, like other young men his age; this was, to an extent, troubling to his parents.

Years had slowly come and gone since Musang joined his parents after spending most of his life with his paternal uncle in Victoria, a beautiful coastal city named after Queen Victoria of England by the first English adventurers who set foot in the area. Every time Musang was around, especially from school, on vacation, he heard the children of the doctrine class chanting their prayers after his father, the catechist, and from time to time, he wondered about some of the things they said. He always wondered why, for example, people always said that God knows everything even before things happen. "If this is the case," he had caught himself wondering aloud from time to time, "why then does He allow terrible things to happen to people?" Man's free will, given him by God, according to this same doctrine, is the response those in authority, whom he dared to question, always gave him. If it is man's choice to do what he wants to do, should something go wrong, then God should not be to blame. Even then, he would wonder: "if man has free will, then what is destiny about?" Each time Musang pursued this reasoning, he got lost as it only got more intricate and perplexing. At one time even, his father had reminded him not to forget that this world, as it is today, is not the way God created it or wanted it to be; people's sins have destroyed the world by ushering in all the pain, hurt, and malice. Musang, accordingly, was always willing to push this line of thought aside as matters of faith; he just had to believe everything about God's goodness. With this conviction, Musang found himself always listening to the kids, and it is true he fell in love not only with the way they chanted their prayers but also with the message contained in the words. It is not surprising then that he started looking more at Father Alphonsus, mindful of his way of doing things around the mission, as a kind of role model. Father Alphonsus was a good man and seemed to love the local people of his parish, most of whom he knew by name. In some cases, Father Alphonsus knew members of entire families even: parents, children, uncles, and aunts. In return, the people greatly admired and respected him.

It was another evening and Musang found himself strolling past the room in which the catechumens met for their doctrine classes. In spite of his slim and well-toned athletic build, Musang always walked slowly, a pace that suited his gentle mien and that habit of always taking in the environment whenever he was walking, one of his forms of relaxation. He was on his way to the neatly kept cemetery next to the church, through which he was fond of pacing when in prayers or when simply contemplating the meaning of life and death, when he heard the children singing *Tantum Ergo*. It caused his heart to swell in a strange way towards the priesthood and the idea of man in a relationship with his God. He always enjoyed this song during Benediction with Father Alphonsus' loud voice bellowing out the "Divine Praises" for the Christians to repeat after him even as the enchanting smell of incense rose with the smoke into the air. He smiled and brushed aside the thought as he began, as always, looking at the numerous tombstones. He was, marvelling at the fact that some people had already led their lives until they were dead while here he was still at the dawn of his, and virtually struggling with choices that forever seemed to yield nothing to convince him of God's interest in him as he had always been preached to. He was in the habit of thinking about what he wanted to become as an adult, a question his father had put to him a number of times only to discover that his son was yet to be sure of what he would like his future to be like. He had not even made up his mind yet if he would want to marry and start a family or become a priest. The decision was made more complicated by the subjects that interested him in school. He was good in both science and art subjects, the kind of student the system valued and elevated to the embarrassment and dissatisfaction of the rest by describing them as "all-round" students. The idea was that he, in fact, could be anything he wanted to be because of this cherished "all-roundedness." The nation needed such students more than those who were just science students or, even worse, those who were mainly arts inclined as they presented them as being of little or no use to the nation. As a result, there were moments when he wanted, badly, to become a doctor and other times when he thought of joining the diplomatic corps of his country, and yet at other times when he considered becoming a lawyer; he could be anything with his educational background and disposition. He was not one of those students limited only to the arts or the sciences and so he enjoyed flirting with ideas about what he could become. The priesthood had even crossed his mind on a number of occasions, and he remembered his father saying, even without knowing his thoughts, what a blessing it would be for him to go to confession to his own son someday.

As Musang strolled passed the classrooms up the narrow slope towards St. Anselm's cemetery, it occurred to him that for quite a while he had been longing to visit the South West Province again, that part of the country where he virtually grew up. It was for this reason that the South West, in a sense, felt more like home to him than his native Mankon; this was where he had spent some strategic years of his life. So instead of looking for a holiday job, Musang planned, as the long third term holidays approached, to obtain permission from his parents to visit his old haunts in all those South West townships: Buea, Tiko, Kumba, and Victoria especially. He was going to talk about it to his father today that he seemed to be in a better mood. First, though, he was going to try winning over his mother before confronting his father so that in case of any resistance on the part of his father, his mother would side with him.

By the time Musang approached his mother's kitchen, he still had about three "Hail Mary" beads left to finish his evening rosary. His mother's voice interrupted his prayers.

9

"What are you doing standing there staring at the ground like an orphan?"

"I'm coming, Mother. I'm just trying to complete my rosary."

His mother went about her cooking, stirring the contents a pot here and there while adjusting the flame in both the hearths even as she struggled with the rising smoke that was already blinding, choking, and causing her to cough.

"Mother!" Musang greeted.

"What's on your mind?"

"What makes you think there's something on my mind?"

"I gave you birth, you think that's not enough to make me know you and your temperaments?" asked Mojoko.

"You win, Mom."

"So what's it? You know you are my first husband, and so when you're worried I'm disturbed."

"You don't need to flatter me to get this one out, Mom. That's why I was coming to the kitchen even before Father shows up." Musang paused and stared at his mother who had dropped all what she was doing and was looking at him with an air of expectation.

"So?" she urged him on.

"Mom, I want to visit the South West."

Mojoko went back to her task before answering back, "That's a tough one. Your father will not listen to that."

"I know, but that's why I want you on my side even before I talk to him."

"What makes you think I'll be on your side that easily?"

"Remember you yourself just said it? I'm your first husband."

Mojoko smiled before speaking, "So you think you got me there?"

"Mom, this is important to me. You know I grew up in the South West, and like you, it's only normal for me to want to go back there from time to time to visit friends and were you not an orphan, I could easily have said family. Mom, I long to see those sights that made my childhood; I want to walk by the beach with my feet in the sand, eat *bangaschool*, *couluba* and real number-one mangoes again."

"Even if you had to go, who would you put up with? Your father would want to know."

Musang knew from experience that when his mother started looking for excuses like this, it meant she was for the idea but was trying to see where her husband might want to say "no" to her son's request. "Mom, I'm not a child any longer. The fact that I'm still living with you my parents does not mean all my friends are doing the same. I have a very good friend who's working with Cameroon Bank (Cam Bank) in Victoria; I plan to stay at his place and then only visit Buea, Tiko, and Kumba on different days."

"We'll try and see what your father will say, but you have to be the one to tell him."

"Thanks, Mom."

"Just wait and see first."

"Mom, how often has Father denied me something when you added your voice to mine?"

"Who knows? The times are changing and your father is getting older too."

Just then, Mojoko and Musang could hear Ndzem whistling the hymn "Daily, Daily, Sing to Mary" as he descended the slope towards his house, the house built for the catechist by the church.

"Woman!" Ndzem called out as he always did when he was happy or in a lighter mood and about to tease Mojoko. "Do you have space enough for me in that kitchen?"

"Unless you're no longer my husband, there will always be space for the father of my children in my kitchen."

"You this my Bakweri girl, you know how to make me happy." Ndzem teased his wife. He bent over avoiding the smoke in the air as he stepped into the kitchen and sat on one of the stools across from Mojoko. She had just rubbed her palm across the surface to wipe off any dirt that could be on the stool. "So what's happening?" he asked.

"Your son and I are just chatting. Try this," said Mojoko offering Ndzem a thigh from the huge chicken she was deep-frying.

"So does this chatting have anything to do with me?" asked Ndzem as he munched on his first bite.

"You know his nineteenth birthday is coming up in a week or two; he wants to seize this opportunity to visit with friends and your in-laws."

"Which my in-laws?"

"Oh, so you think because Uncle Mbella, my last surviving relative who gave me to you in marriage died, I'm now without people? Remember that I am Mojoko, daughter of the sea, and the Bakweri are my people. Your son wants to go to the South West to visit the places where he grew up," added Mojoko without waiting for Ndzem to react.

"How would he go? Where would he put up? Has he thought of these things?"

"Yes, he has," answered Mojoko.

"I see, so you people had everything planned out and you were just waiting to slaughter me if I should say otherwise, is that not so?"

"Husband, that is not the point. The fact is that no matter what we plan or intend to do, if you do not approve of it, we cannot feel good about it; your permission is always priority."

"Well, let me eat something first; we can talk about that later." Ndzem never gave in to his wife directly, but Musang knew better that when his father postponed issues raised by his mother, he was indirectly giving in to her request. He was going to go on with his arrangements: call his friend, and then pull out of his bank account some of his allowance, which he had been saving for moments like this. He would leave for Victoria in under a week and spend at least a month with his friend.

Chapter 2

It was about 3:00pm when the Peugeot 404 station wagon with the business name Buea-Bamenda written on the carriage, which Musang had taken as his means of transportation, rolled into the city of Victoria. It went past the Provincial Hospital on the right and down into Half Mile where it came to a halt in the premises of a Shell petrol station for the passengers to disembark. Drivers, more often than not, preferred dropping off passengers out here at the Shell Petrol filling station instead of going into the Bus Station reserved for passengers and transport vehicles going in and out of town. They went into the Bus Station only when they were making a return trip almost immediately, in which case they went in to get a number in line since the vehicles took turns loading following these numbers. It was illegal to do otherwise or to be found picking up passengers from beyond the Bus Station confines. One after the other the passengers emerged, stretching as they looked around, taking in Victoria. Since he was going in his direction, the driver courteously dropped Musang off a short distance to the Victoria High Court next to where Musang's friend, Brandon, was living, then zoomed off towards Bota.

Brandon had gone to work, but the last time they spoke on the phone, he had informed Musang of where he would leave his key. It was a long building, only a room's width in depth, and about four rooms in length. It was built of blocks and was never plastered, nor was it painted. The grey blocks were designed such that it was obvious there had been no intention of painting the building after it was completed. Musang retrieved the key from under a nearby stone, unlocked and swung open the door. He was impressed by virtually everything about his friend's little apartment. To his right was a beautiful dining table covered with a reddish tablecloth with some flower markings. In order to create space, Brandon had brought the table really close to the only window in the parlour facing the front of the house where a lush hibiscus hedge was sprawling. It kept a small bush at bay and the back of neighbouring houses out of sight. Unless one deliberately stood on one's toes to see beyond the hedge, only then did a small unkempt lawn and the back of nearby compounds come into view. Brandon's house looked like one of those smaller buildings for servants that colonial administrations built close to the homes of colonial administrators, but there was no master's lodge anywhere in sight to confirm this suspicion. Beyond the dining table and further into the parlour, Brandon had a beautiful set of red chairs with thick comfortable cushions. In the centre stood a sturdy glass-top coffee table with a tablecloth of the same design and colour like the one on the dining table. There was a note for Musang on the coffee table. Brandon was welcoming him to Victoria and instructing him to join him at the bank just before it was 6:00pm. From the parlour, another door led into the bedroom; it was a one-bedroom apartment. Musang walked into the room and into the aroma of a mixture of cologne and perfume. He looked around and smiled to himself when he saw some female dresses in the closet. "They must belong to Brandon's girlfriend," he thought to himself. Musang set his bag in one corner of the closet, stared at the huge and well-made bed before stepping out into the parlour where he crashed into a chair enjoying the newfound freedom: just he and his friend out in the South West without his parents or people who knew him.

"This will be fun," he said aloud as he leaned his head against the welcoming cushions.

When Musang started, he realized he had snoozed for about an hour. He quickly jumped into the shower, had a change of clothes, and was on his way to the bank where Brandon worked. It was 5:50 pm when Musang got to the bank, so he decided to wait outside for his friend who had already seen him through a window and was waving. It was too good to be true: Musang was in Victoria after about five years. He spun around on his heels as he took in deep breaths of the refreshing Atlantic breeze that wafted itself by at this time of the evening. It was the same Cameroon Bank stone building, just freshly painted, the stones black and the network of cement between the stones white. Bay Salon Hotel was still comfortably perched on the knoll from the Centenary Stadium and across from the bank as always, but the road that went past directly in front of the hotel had been re-routed. The road now went past, following the roundabout, and then joined the road to the bank, only to turn left suddenly and up a short but steep slope onto the premises of Bay Salon Hotel. It then meandered past into a new neighbourhood that was just sprouting behind the hotel. Musang thought of the days when he used to stand by Bay Hotel to listen to the hotel's live band churning out the latest music of those days – "Funky Four Corners," "Mr. Big Stuff," "I'll Take You There," and so on, and then at night he would hear goats screaming to death as they were slaughtered for the menu. His mind was still coughing up scenes from the past when Brandon called out.

"*L'homme!*"

Musang spun around on his heels to see his friend neatly dressed as always, but this time he had on a tie. Musang, immediately, knew it had to be bank policy, for Brandon hated ties. "*L'homme!*" Musang answered in return. Brandon, some inches taller and a shade or two darker in hue than Musang, walked with his head always slightly lowered from the neck level, which gave him a slight premature hunch to his back. Young people who walked with this hunch were described as arrogant, an assumption which belied Brandon's easy-going nature. He looked unapproachable, indeed, but this was because he was shy rather than haughty. They laughed and hugged as Brandon introduced Musang to his friends, male and female, who were still just coming out of the bank. They shook his hand casually with a quick "hello" or "welcome" and walked past with a promise to see him some other time.

Then, the girl who was locking the door of the bank turned around. Brandon giggled as he heard Musang gasp and curse under his breath because of her beauty. She smiled at them from a distance revealing brilliantly white teeth and a tiny gap between her two upper incisors. She had on a cream white long sleeve blouse that revealed vaguely, in a tantalizing manner, the outline of her bra around her body. Each breast was the size of half a pineapple with pointed tips that seemed to crush against her breast-wear from within. "Hello!" she greeted Musang, with her smile broadening as she stretched out her right hand, which Musang took in his. "My name is Etonde," she said in a slightly coarse voice, as if a cough was coming on, which was barely audible.

"Musang! Musang Ngang Tijie is my name, and it's a pleasure meeting you." Musang was looking directly into her eyes.

"Nice meeting you too. Your first time in Victoria?"

"Na-aaa! This is my town; I grew up here."

"Oh, I see," answered Etonde as she threw back the upper part of her torso and took another look at Musang's face, displaying a kind of pleasant surprise.

"Yes, yes, but it's obvious so much has changed in the years I have been away." Musang spoke as he scanned the surrounding landscape casually, his eyes sweeping past the hill on which stood the District Officer's residence until his gaze got back to the bank building, and then into Etonde's eyes.

"That's true, in any case," confirmed Etonde returning Musang's gaze. "It was good talking to you," she added after a brief pause.

"The pleasure was mine."

"Hello, and I'm Brandon," said Brandon in jest, since it had all been Musang and Etonde exchanging pleasantries as if there was nobody else around but the two of them.

"Hello! Are you new here or is Victoria your town too?" Etonde teased him, and they all laughed aloud. "Okay see you guys later on. I guess you and your friend are joining us later on tonight, right?"

"Sure," Brandon answered, "it is even his birthday today, that is if my memory serves me right, so there will be a lot of celebrating, but first I need to get him to eat."

"Of course," returned Etonde as she smiled and walked away with gentle yet poised strides that caused her slightly bulging hips to swing from side to side in her just tight enough skirt, which revealed her curves provocatively. Through the slit at the back of the skirt, exactly above the back of her knees, Musang could see her complexion and the texture of her body; it was soft and beckoning. Her strides were confident and calculated; those of a young woman who knew the effect her body and structure had on men each time she walked passed. Musang looked at her ankles closely, yes, just what he likes in a woman—just about enough flesh around the ankles but not that much to pass for fat.

"*L'homme*!" Brandon called out to Musang in a state of disbelief. "Man, you're already selling like hot cake!"

"What do you mean?"

"*L'homme*, that's a girl virtually every guy in this bank has tried dating in vain. She is quiet, yes, polite, and friendly even, yet in a strange way distant. She speaks to us her colleagues out of professional courtesy alone, it would seem, and all of a sudden, she sounds like she knows me so well and we are so close just because she has seen you? This is not possible!"

"What makes you think she's sounding like that just because she's seen me?" asked Musang with a smile hovering on the edge of his mouth.

"How long do you think I've been working with this girl? It's about a year today and each time somebody asks her out, it's one excuse or another, until we've all given up. She claims we're her brothers. I've tried making this girl to understand that my sisters are all in Bamenda, but she just laughs at me instead."

Musang smiled quietly as his mind reviewed the picture of the girl he had just seen. Her eyes struck him as interesting: brilliantly black pupils against a calm white background, which conjured a certain gentleness that contradicted the strength of character she had just revealed. He felt a strange sense of joy overwhelm his being as he thought of their pending encounter that evening. He could not wait to see her again. "She's a very beautiful girl," he confirmed as Brandon stared at him with disbelief written all over his face.

"This is not possible!" Brandon still could not belief the interest, masqueraded as courtesy, which Etonde had shown his friend, Musang, upon their very first encounter. "*L'homme*,

20

let's go, Man. We'll get something to eat and then we would hang out for a while before going back home; after all, it is Friday night and we do not work on Saturdays."

It was 11:00 pm when Brandon and Musang sauntered into the nightclub section of Park Hotel Miramar. The music was blasting and the bass pounding away at one's heart, with lights of every shade flashing and splashing all over the place. Brandon, from habit, looked over at the section to his right with soft comfortable couches where he and his colleagues usually sat on such evenings, and there indeed they were. As he walked over, Musang followed as if reluctantly and in the process taking in the entire dance floor scene and rating it. It was worth the while. There were pairs and small groups of well-dressed young men and women dancing happily to some of the latest music, obviously celebrating their youth and the weekend. Finally, Musang brought his eyes to rest on the group with members of which he was now exchanging handshakes, and there she was again. Etonde sat at one edge of a love seat with another male colleague on the other end, and since it would have been a little too tight for the duo to join them, Brandon and Musang, after shaking hands, walked over to the counter where they sat on high stools sipping at their drinks. From time to time, Brandon went to the dance floor with one tipsy girl after another; it was obvious to Musang the girls around town knew him well. All evening, although Musang did not go over to chat with Etonde, he could barely take his eyes off her blithe body, and he made it obvious to her that he had his eyes on her. She had on a red gown that hung from thin straps at the shoulders and flared into a loose bottom with countless pleats that seemed to trickle down until just below her knees, showing off her well-shaped legs. Her shoes were black high heels with broad but short delicate velvet-looking straps that she had buckled round her firm ankles. Each time she walked to the counter to get herself a drink, Musang liked the way her hips would bulge seductively on the sides, causing the pleats to lose their disciplined lines temporarily, widening against her hips like the scales on a python's body after it has swallowed a huge meal. From time to time Etonde looked his way, and in spite of the eye contact, Musang refused walking over to ask her for a dance. He chose to remain somewhat perplexing rather than give away too much of himself on this very first day. If this girl was as hard to get as Brandon was assuring him, then he had to take his time and come across as the serious person that he is and not like somebody just out for a fling. In fact, Musang was a one-man-one-woman kind of person and just did not rush into relationships. His guiding principle was that he dated only girls he would not hesitate getting married to, should it become necessary. Accordingly, he studied his girls well before making any move.

The night seemed to be warming up, although it was already 1:00am, when Musang told Brandon he was feeling tired and wanted to go back home. Brandon laughed at his friend; he was used to his strict ways and the fact that he was not one who hung out late, nor did he drink that much alcohol either. "*L'homme*, things are just beginning to warm up and you want to go home? I was thinking from here we would go to New Town for you to eat some chicken."

"Don't worry about that today. I've only just arrived and we've quite a while ahead of us."

"Okay, I'll get a taxi for you outside. You want to let my friends know you're leaving?"

"If it's necessary, then just let them know I had to sneak out because I didn't want to dampen their evening. Tell Etonde I said I was tired and needed to rest."

When Brandon returned into the nightclub after seeing off Musang, he noticed Etonde eyeing him casually, but he did not miss the question in her gaze, so he decided to announce Musang's message to the group. He then inched in closer and told Etonde in her ears what Musang had said. Etonde pulled her head back and with a smile stared at Brandon in the eyes as if to say why single me out? Nevertheless, they both understood the fact that something special was brewing between Musang and her no matter how neutral they both pretended to be.

A whole week had gone by since the night at Miramar and Musang had not seen Etonde, but his heart was with her all the time, for he spent his lonely hours, when Brandon was at work, thinking of her. He had found out everything about Etonde from Brandon and the more he found out, the more he admired her. It was Friday again and as Brandon left the house to go to work, Musang extended an invitation to Etonde. "*L'homme*, tell Etonde I said I'd like her to stop over tomorrow at noon."

"But we would be with them tonight?" Brandon queried.

"No, I will not be there. Just tell her that for me, Man."

"Okay, Abakwa Boy!" answered Brandon referring to Musang's Grassfield roots like they usually did when they wanted to tease each other.

Musang smiled quietly as Brandon walked away to work.

Later that night when Brandon returned and Musang asked, all Brandon could say was that he gave her Musang's message.

"So what did she say?"

"Nothing! I told her what you said, and then immediately went on to explain how to get to my house. She just looked at me and went about what she was doing. It was at work." Brandon pointed out before adding as he tried to be consoling, "*L'homme*, I told you we can't figure that chap out, Man. Everyone here has tried and failed, even our controllers from Douala with all the money they show up here willing to spend. We cannot seem to tell what she wants in a man or if she's even thinking about men."

Musang smiled as he looked on in the distance without uttering a word. He was wondering if he had misinterpreted the look in Etonde's eyes when they first met, but his mind told him he was right: he had seen suppressed admiration and he was sure his disposition was also keeping her on edge. He has not rushed in just because she looks so beautiful and sounds very smart; he has taken his time. He smiled gently as he accused himself in the manner of another girl whom he had missed dating in Douala. Mercy was a beautiful girl from Mamfe who lived with another female friend somewhere near *Ecole Publique de Bepanda*. When Musang's friend Claude had introduced them to each other for the first time, it was obvious they both fell for each other, but Musang, as usual, took his time. Unable to take the stress, one day Mercy cornered Musang in the corridor leading out of their flat, pinned him against the wall with her body, and accused him of being slow. Yes, he was slow, but he would rather be slow and sure than rush into things and make a fool of himself.

It was already late morning, and Saturday was promising to be a beautiful day with the bright rays of the sun landing on part of the hedge outside, the other half still under the building's shadow. Musang, with both his legs stretched onto the coffee table, was already sitting in the parlour and reading

Plain Truth, an international news magazine, when Brandon joined him from the bedroom. They talked about Brandon's activities of the night before and how their group had ended up in New Town where some beautiful girls own a Chicken Parlour where they had eaten chicken and drunk so much dry gin such that he could not even remember how he got back home. Musang encouraged him to drink a lot of water and to take a shower; he was sure the water would help dilute the alcohol in his veins while the shower would freshen him.

Brandon was still in the shower when he heard the footsteps and then the voices. He paused in the process of lathering his body and listened keenly; it was Etonde greeting Musang. He could not believe his ears. He looked at his watch, which he had placed on the windowsill when he realized he had brought it into the shower, and it was midday. Brandon quickly dried himself and tied the towel around his waist. He had no choice, as there was no other way by which he could get into his bedroom without going through the parlour where Etonde was now sitting and chatting idly with Musang.

"Wow!" Brandon exclaimed with a faked start at the threshold upon seeing Etonde, pretending not to have known she was there. "I'm sorry I'm just getting out of the shower. How're you?"

Etonde smiled gently as she greeted in response, "I'm fine Billy," she answered, calling Brandon the way everyone at the bank called him. "How come you're still taking your bath this late in the day?"

"First of all, I'm a bachelor and so I can do whatever I like whenever," replied Brandon laughing.

"I'm sorry I didn't know that," Etonde teased him.

"And secondly," continued Brandon, "I'm still just getting out of bed now after all of yesterday's activities." Brandon was talking and laughing as he walked on into the bedroom in disbelief. Musang followed Brandon into the bedroom as if to tell him "I told you!" They exchanged looks and Brandon motioned to Musang that he was dangerous by wagging his right index finger repeatedly at him. They chuckled furtively just as Brandon gestured to him, with his right hand, to hurry back into the parlour so Etonde would not think they were talking about her. He joined them a few minutes later on feeling fresh and smelling good: his favourite cologne brand – Givenchy.

"So, Etonde, how're you today, and were my directions good?" It was Brandon.

"I'm fine, thank you. Yes, you did a pretty good job with your directions, although I had to figure out on my own which way to go after the taxi dropped me off under that tree behind there."

"Yeah! Well…. I've invited you repeatedly to my house ever since I first met you, but you won't come, so tell me, what it is this *Graffi* boy did to make you come?"

Etonde smiled broadly, as she answered back jokingly and knowing she was not telling the truth. "You've never invited me to your house," she teased.

"Maybe you don't know I am *Graffi* also?" Brandon teased.

"It has nothing to do with being *Graffi* -" Etonde answered still smiling.

Brandon cut in, "Don't worry, I'm just kidding; it's good and quite an honour to have you with us."

"Thank you," answered Etonde genuinely impressed. She was smiling and rocking herself from her waist up with her left knee in both her palms and her fingers interwoven.

"*L'homme*, I will be back shortly; I just want to check a few things out here in Gardens." Brandon spoke as he placed the last bottle of drink on the table. There was coke, Top Citron, tonic, and an unopened bottle of Gordon's Dry Gin with an unopened packet of biscuits. "Okay, see you guys in a while." Brandon stepped out. Musang was sure, Brandon's girlfriend, Maggie, was Brandon's only business in Gardens at this hour of the day. Maggie was a lovely, gentle woman but without Brandon's nocturnal qualities as they were always quarrelling because she kept trying to prevent Brandon from squandering his money, especially when he was out late at night, on what she considered nonsense.

"Thanks for coming," Musang spluttered after Brandon walked out.

"Thanks for inviting me over," Etonde answered back with so much ease.

"I have heard so much about you."

"About me?" asked Etonde genuinely surprised.

Musang nodded.

"From whom?"

"Brandon!"

"What does he know about me?" It was almost a sneer, but she was joking.

"You would be surprised, a lot besides the fact that you work at Cam Bank with him. For example, you went to Saker, then CCAS Kumba, and did very well in all your major exams, for which reason the bank readily employed you. You are also planning on going overseas to further your education-"

"I am sure he knows when and where I was born also."

"I will not be surprised," Musang was smiling. "What matters is that he holds you in such high esteem."

"I'm flattered."

"I'm sure you know better than that."

By the time Brandon returned with his girlfriend Maggie, who had a basket in her hand, Musang and Etonde were so better acquainted. In fact, Brandon was in denial when he walked in and saw Etonde standing and staring out to the back of his yard with Musang next to her. He was standing directly behind and leaning against her back with both his arms imprisoning Etonde, somewhat, with his fingers clamped around the metal security bars, about five inches apart, running the parallel length of the window through which they were both gazing. Brandon noticed that Etonde's hands rested on Musang's which hemmed her in. Etonde turned her face past Musang's, to greet Brandon, but when she saw Maggie walking in after him. She walked out gently from behind Musang's body to greet her. They spent the rest of the day talking, eating, drinking and making light conversation. Maggie could not help laughing at Brandon's disbelief that Etonde gave in to a man.

"What does Billy mean by 'give in to a man'? Is there anything wrong with seeing a man you admire and becoming friends with him?" asked Etonde smiling incredulously at the big deal seemingly being made about the fact that she was falling for Musang.

"So before this *Graffi* boy came into town you never saw anyone you admired?" joked Brandon.

"*L'homme!*" Etonde, trying hard to oblige Brandon to reason with her, called Brandon the way Musang called him. Taken by surprise, they all burst out laughing at the influence

Musang had over her already. Etonde went on, "Women look at things differently, and what you think may appeal to a woman may not necessarily."

"So true," Maggie confirmed.

"Could you leave Etonde alone?" Musang interjected.

"Oh, I'm sorry *Sar*," Brandon joked.

It was 6:00pm when Maggie and Etonde stood up, as if on cue, to let Brandon and Musang know it was time to go.

"But the two of you can't leave at once, you didn't come in at the same time," protested Musang. "You have to go the way you came in, which means Etonde who came in first will leave, and then some hours after, Maggie who came in second can leave."

"Don't forget that I just came in to bring the two of you something to eat." Observed Maggie. "When I'm visiting, you will not just keep me in doors like today; should Etonde happen to be here, then you will have to take us out."

"As much as I would like to have them stay around much longer, I must say, they both have spent quite some time with us. We don't want a situation where next time they'll just refuse showing up because we won't let them go when it is time for them to leave."

"You're right. In that case, we better see them off."

Because Maggie's home was not far away, they all walked there to see her off, then took a taxi to Sokolo to see off Etonde where she was living with her siblings and her parents. Musang and Brandon did not get out of the taxi so as not to betray Etonde's company to her family—not that it mattered—who must have been looking from behind those glass windows when the taxi pulled up and came to a stop at the junction where the road branches off into their compound.

"Thanks for a wonderful day gentlemen," said Etonde as she made to get out of the taxi. Sandwiched, she turned to her right and hugged Brandon before turning to her left to stare at Musang in his eyes for a while. She then gave Musang a quick peck on his jaw before squeezing past him and out of the taxi. She walked away without another word. As the taxi took off, they continued staring at her as she strode briskly down the driveway to their home. Then Brandon gave Musang this nasty look, which betrayed his admiration for Musang's accomplishment.

"*L'homme*, you are a tough guy, Man. I knew you were tough but not this tough. You don't know what you have in your hands."

"I know!"

"How I wish tomorrow was Monday so I could look at her at work and wonder if indeed it is the same Etonde, the same girl I've been working with who would not listen to any of our avowals of the love we have and feel for her. Is she coming tomorrow?"

"No, she and her parents are going to Buea for a *born-house* at Long Street."

"Who gave birth?"

"How would I know?"

"You did not ask?"

"To do what with that information?"

"Well, you still have about two weeks left, and, of course, if things turn out to be as serious as I am predicting, then she can also always come to Bamenda to visit you."

"That's true."

The night was getting darker and quieter as they enjoyed their conversation without realizing how far back into town they had come. The taxi driver was just going past Rivoli

Cinema on the left when he spoke up: "So where exactly do I drop you off gentlemen?

"Just here at Gardens!" Brandon called out. "We are sorry we got carried away."

"Nothing to worry about; who wouldn't be after seeing off such a beautiful lady?"

"Thanks," Musang said to the driver, as he paid him off, before picking his way in the dark after Brandon who was already climbing the gentle slope leading to his house.

To Brandon and Musang, the remaining weeks of his vacation went by like a breath of fresh air. It was all fun, and spending time in much loved company caused Musang to delay his return trip to Bamenda by two days. At Etonde's work, people wondered at this newfound friendship with Brandon, but nobody could come out clean to ask. She now called Brandon "*L'homme,*" no longer "Billy" like every other colleague. Furthermore, both of them now spent virtually every free second at work or breaktime together. Musang moved his departure date which fell on a Friday to Sunday so that Etonde would be somewhat free to see him off at the Bus Station.

Sunday came at last. Musang hated travelling on Sundays since, more often than not, it meant missing Mass if he took off early to get to his destination in good time. This time, however, he was returning to Bamenda, his town, and it did not matter how late he got there, so he went to Mass first before leaving for the Bus Station. At last, there they stood all three together—Musang, Brandon, and Etonde—chatting and whiling time, waiting for the bus to fill up with passengers so Musang could be on his way. Musang's back was leaning against the bus and Etonde against his body in an embrace, with the side of her head against his chest, her hands around his waist and his left arm wrapped about her shoulder as they waited. There was room in the vehicle for just one more passenger, then after about twenty minutes, it was time to depart with the arrival of a young mother with her screaming baby, on her way to Bamenda. Musang promised to call often and that over the phone they would make plans that are more concrete. It was the first time Brandon had seen Etonde kiss Musang on the lips in a genuinely romantic fashion; it was always a quick smack on his jaw and it was over, like the night they saw her off at Sokolo. Musang sank into his seat and she slammed the door shut. As they rolled out of the park, Musang saw Etonde walking hand in hand with Brandon; she needed the support. Musang waved goodbye, but only Brandon waved back as their fourteen-seater bus gathered speed past Half-Mile and up the slope towards Mile 1 and out of Victoria.

Chapter 3

A whole week had gone by since Musang returned from Victoria before he could find the time to sit and chat with his mother about his trip. He told her about his friend Brandon and the wonderful reception he gave him. He also elaborated on the fact that Brandon did not have a pot in his house, and so they had to eat restaurant food on a daily basis, which got Mojoko laughing hard. When he started talking to his mother about Etonde, Mojoko stopped what she was doing and looked at her son in the eye.

"You like her?" She exclaimed, after listening to him for a while, in a manner that was also a question at the same time.

"Yes, Mom. She is not only pretty, she is kind, gentle, and generous, and with a certain air about her that I like very much."

"Now that she is from the South West, I do not know what your father's people will think."

"What do you mean by what my father's people would think? What would they think? Are they the ones getting married?"

"My son, it is not as easy as it may seem. You know, tradition is something that runs deep. For your father, he certainly won't mind, but his family is likely to think I am behind this—trying to carry their grandson away to the coast as I have carried their son."

"Mom, people still think like that these days?"

"I am afraid so, Son. You will not believe this, but there are paternal aunts of yours who still do not want to see me, even after all these years that I have been married to their brother. They say I am squandering his money and sending what I cannot consume down to the coast. I keep asking myself where the money they are talking about is from. One would think their brother is a medical doctor or still the businessman he used to be, instead of a catechist who has to struggle all the time just to make ends meet. They don't get it; they don't get the fact that it was his character, the kind heart that I could tell he has, of all his friends and even the wealthier suitors who came for me that won my heart over to him."

"But Mom, you know in-laws are always like that, no matter where they come from. Who knows what your parents and relatives would have been saying were they alive today?"

"I hear you, but I am particularly worried because, again, you are the first son of your father's, and so his people would want you to marry a girl from Mankon."

"Mom, enough of that kind of talk; I've told you I will marry wherever my heart leads me."

"I hear you, Son, but to go against your people like that, you would have to develop a thick skin. And I don't advise it because family is always family no matter what."

"In so far as you and dad are going to be happy, I'm fine."

"No, Musang, it can never be like that. We are a family people, and so family always comes first. The thing to say is that we'll do all to win their approval, okay! Go now, go and get ready for your trip. With God, you will get a passport, and those Americans will give you a visa, unless God wishes otherwise for you. Make sure all your documents are together, and remember, as they say it, when you are talking to a white man look him in the eyes. Those people have no sense of respect: a child will be talking to the father and looking at him in the eyes as if they are equals."

34

"Their argument, I hear, and which we learned in our culture class, is that to them everybody is equal before the law, something that makes me laugh each time I hear it. If they believed in that, how is it that they went around buying and selling human beings as if they were selling animals and even their own courts could not get them to stop without a fight? In fact, it took the use of soldiers to enforce the laws that brought about a semblance of change to the slave era."

"Anyway, also remember what your father has always said: those people hate liars, so tell them the truth and look into their eyes without fear. After all, that's what they want, so defy them if it will get you what you're out for."

"Good night, Father," Musang called after his father as he walked out of his son's room where they had been talking about his activities for the coming week. His father had ended up wishing him well and calling on the ancestors to go with him. Musang fell asleep thinking of Etonde. He had spoken to her earlier on in the day and told her of his upcoming trip to the embassy and she was very happy for him, but she complained about how she was missing him.

As Ndzem walked out of Musang's room, he was of the opinion that something was wrong, but he could not put his finger on it as Musang seemed happy but somewhat preoccupied. "Maybe it was the approaching struggle to acquire a Cameroonian passport and the impending interview at the US embassy following which his application for a US visa could be accepted or rejected that was getting to him," he wondered.

It was 4:00 am when Musang got to the Yaounde Taxi Park to find a vehicle for the capital city. He wanted to use one of those newer *Dina* buses with all the passengers sitting and facing in front, instead of those older models with the

35

passengers behind sitting and facing each other as if being transported in a military truck. Again, he wanted to get to the immigration police as early as possible and then he could make it to the US embassy before it was noon if he was lucky enough to get a passport booklet right away. He was of the conviction that being the capital, the main source of the booklets, it should not take him that long to get his passport since he had sent a completed dossier with all the requirements two weeks in advance. Accordingly, he pictured a situation where he would arrive and within an hour pick up his passport and proceed to the US embassy. He hated spending any time in Yaounde with the rather disrespectful and somewhat chaotic attitude displayed by the characteristically distant occupants of the city as opposed to the calm, gentle, and respectful approach he was used to back home in Bamenda with people acknowledging each other all the time. Back in Bamenda, people show they recognize someone even from a previous visit and can even chat, but this had not been his experience in Yaounde each time he had visited. People just seemed preoccupied with one thing or the other and barely exchanged greetings. He had heard it was a disease of the cities. The result was that he unknowingly developed a dislike for the city as a whole. Whenever he was there, he just wanted to be done with whatever brought him to Yaounde and then leave. It was the same feeling that he was already experiencing that was making him uncomfortable as he stepped out of the bus from Bamenda.

"Taxi!" Musang called out before shouting out his destination as the driver slowed down. "*Police des Frontières!*"

The taxi came to a complete stop. "*Montez!*" The driver called out in French.

36

Musang boarded, and the driver sped off. The scene before him was disturbing: there were bikers, many without helmets in case of an accident, swerving dangerously in and out of traffic at breakneck speed. Some of the young riders, seemingly dazed, curved proudly behind the handlebars of rusty old bikes as if riding was quite an achievement, were transporting women with babies strapped to their backs. Just then, another young man with a worn-out light reflecting jacket sped by with an aluminium pot on his head for a helmet. The woman he carried behind balanced a similar pot on the edge of her headtie, not intending to ruffle her scarf and hair. The pedestrians by the roadside were completely at a loss as to how to manoeuvre their way across such insane traffic. This was happening even as police officers in uniform idled around nonchalantly, seemingly looking for something else in particular.

"Madness!" Musang hissed aloud in defiance of the scene before him. His mind flashed back to the good old days when one could walk around with vehicles making way for pedestrians. Now a third category of users was vying with dazed pedestrians for the roads—untrained bikers risking the lives of citizens as they ferried others from one location to another within the city of Yaounde. Once upon a time, there were beautiful buses transporting people from one neighbourhood to the next for a trite. How such a transportation corporation with a service so incredibly highly in demand collapsed remains one of the country's many financial puzzles. Just then, Musang saw a signboard with *"L'Ambassade de France"* neatly written on it, with an arrow pointing towards Bastos, a neighbourhood occupied by the wealthy. "These bastards are still in control here," he thought to himself, "else why are there directions to the French embassy and not to the almighty American embassy which receives thousands more visa-seeking-Cameroonians on a weekly basis than the French embassy?" he pondered. It was then it occurred to Musang that lately he was no longer seeing those French men in Cameroon's military uniforms driving jeeps arrogantly along the streets. It was good he was planning to leave Cameroon for a long time if he could get his visa from the US embassy. He was completely fed up with all the nonsense happening in his country with the people remaining as passive as if all was well. "How is it that a child is born, raised until he gets married and is having his own children and the same individual is in place as head of state with other morons ready to dance and fête with every opportunity of the buffoon's appearance in public?" Musang could not wait to see for himself how free the free world, as the United States of America is always presented in the news, would be, nor could he wait to experience the opportunities in the land of opportunities, another popular term of reference for the United States. The furthest the taxi could approach the immigration office was about two hundred feet away because of some repairs taking place in the street where the tar had come off leaving behind huge dusty undulations and deep potholes in certain areas.

Foremost on his mind, however, was the challenge of getting a Cameroonian passport in order to be able to travel; a procedure that was comparable to the biblical camel going through the eye of a needle for the poor and ordinary in society, like him. Accordingly, for Musang to get a passport would be nothing short of a miracle. Hemmed in thus, the dictator in office was determined and convinced Cameroonians would not easily come by subversive ideas since the radio, especially, fed them only ideas with which the government wanted them nourished.

As Musang walked on, taking in the noisy scene before him, marked by an unfortunate aura of chaos, confusion, and apathy, something welled up inside of him, leaving a bitter taste in his mouth. It was a feeling he always experienced each time he visited major French speaking towns, especially Yaounde, the capital city of his country where from time to time people from other regions are made to feel unwelcome by the locals. Besides the locals worthless arrogance towards other citizens forced to come to Yaounde because of the centralized and frustratingly inefficient administrative system in place, Musang's repeated discovery of the biased bilingual structure of the country is what usually provokes this feeling of disgust towards Yaounde. For example, Musang easily noticed that everything, except on government buildings, was written only in French, whereas in all Anglophone cities or towns, virtually everything written in English was again repeated in French for the benefit of the French speaking Cameroonian. He had always wondered what this was all about: the simple numerical advantage the Francophone population had over the Anglophones, or some idiotic scheme towards slowly turning Anglophones into third generation Francophones, recolonized this time by a state within their twin-state federation of Anglophone and Francophone Cameroons. Musang was still mumbling his dissatisfaction at the kind of bilingualism practiced in his country when his eyes landed on the sign on the front roof of a funny looking stone building on which appeared the letters "*Police des Frontières.*" He was coming to see the commissioner himself to apply for a passport since the immigration office in Bamenda had told him they were out of booklets. Otherwise,

Musang would never set foot in this city with its fake lifestyle: a city where virtually everyone is a victim of some form of egomania. Just about everybody one meets wants to be considered very important and equally high up the social ladder. Interestingly, this is in spite of how broke, exploited, and abused the majority are but for the hand-me-down and worn out used suits in which they are always parading with much unmerited airs, bloated balloons that can easily be popped into worthlessness by the slightest financial pressure. As he approached it, Musang took in the building with a couple of swift movements of his eyes in the manner of a painter's brush, from side to side. From outside, it did not look that beautiful, nor was it imposing. At the door, just to the right and before the threshold, sat a lone man in civilian attire with a faraway gaze in his eyes like a man wondering about the source of his next meal.

"Good morning," greeted Musang.

There was no reply.

"I am here to apply for a passport."

Still no reply; the statue's eyes moved with disgust in its gaze as it sized Musang from his feet to his head and back down to his feet.

It occurred to Musang that this must be one of those Francophones without knowledge of a single English word, so he switched into French and repeated his greeting. He was just about going on to explain why he was there when the contraption snapped; the mute spoke up in French, and with a lot of anger.

"You came and were speaking in English; you think that's what we eat here?"

Instead of feeling hurt or insulted, Musang was totally at a loss at such a display from a police officer as he had deduced

40

the man was. Musang smiled in disbelief and at the same time wondered when this seething anger and seeming hate was brewed. He was convinced it could not have been just between the time he approached the building and greeted the man else, he must be a very bitter person naturally. He looked skinny, a kind of a drunk with cigarette stained lips and knuckles. Musang was still smiling as the man fumed, in his mind imagining a hen-pecked husband who had carried his fight with his wife along with him to work. Then it occurred to him it must be a combination of this and the man's hate for either English or English speaking Cameroonians. Still smiling, Musang answered back: "If I am not mistaken, I am still in Cameroon, and I believe Cameroon is said to be a bilingual country?" It was more of a statement than a question. "However, when I realized you did not seem to understand a word of English, I had to switch to French. Is there a crime in that?" The angry man was still fuming and gazing at Musang with a look as if had he his way he could not even tell what he would do to him. Musang decided to ignore this bitter specimen of a Cameroonian and with a calm and condescending smile walked on into the building and immediately into an area accommodating about eight other police officers, men and women in uniform sitting behind work desks.

"Why do you people have such an angry officer welcoming people into your office?"

Everyone looked up but nobody said a word. Just then, his eyes fell on the nametag on one of the desks and he could tell it was a name from around Kumba within the English speaking part of the country. He approached the young woman Miss Jikam and asked for help with applying for a passport. Miss Jikam pointed out to another officer sitting a couple of desks away from her and asked Musang to go see him. The officer concerned had seen Miss Jikam sending him over. He pulled out some forms, which he dumped in front of Musang, and asked him to fill them out. About twenty minutes had elapsed by the time Musang was done filling out the forms. He pushed them back in front of the officer who stared at the bunch with a quizzical look in his eyes as if he could not understand what Musang was doing. Musang stared back at him equally lost.

"You are from the province. Did you send an application package before coming?"

"About two weeks ago," answered Musang.

"Well then," The policeman concluded, come back next week.

"I cannot come back next week. I do not live in Yaounde. As you can see from my forms, I am all the way from Bamenda and I have nobody with whom to spend the night here in Yaounde; I can barely afford my hotel bill for a night.

"Well, you can try tomorrow," the officer mumbled emphasizing the word "try."

"Thank you," Musang said aloud as he stood up, and then thanked Miss Jikam before turning and walking out ignoring the threat still sitting by the door. "An idiot," he said under his breath hoping the threat heard him, yet hoping he did not. He did not mind the fact that they had asked him to return the next day instead of after a whole week because he was determined not to give them a single franc as bribe.

It was a new day. By the time Musang had his passport in his hand the day before, it was already too late for him to venture to the US embassy. He had gone home to his secondary school mate's house at Melen quarters where he was putting up. His determination was to get to the US

42

embassy the next morning before it was 9:00am. "Those Americans are very strict about time, and usually there is always a large number of people already waiting by mid-day, all wanting to get a visa to the US," he thought. His mind conjured up mental pictures of what it could be like in the United States. His maternal uncle in Oklahoma, Vincent, had always written back that it was beautiful out there and each time he wrote, he sent scores of pictures of himself, his car, and one girl or another in beautiful houses or outside on carefully manicured lawns. Musang did not seem to care about all those things. His only reason for wanting to go to the US was the fact that he had been told an academic degree from the US would be recognized anywhere in the world; otherwise, he would not leave a girl like Etonde behind for any reason whatsoever. At the worst, he could start a small business of his own and lead a reasonably good life. He was convinced going to Nigeria would also give him a good degree that would equally be recognized anywhere in the world. After all, what with those great universities there and those distinguished professors he had heard so much about whose books he was even using in his Physics and Chemistry classes, professors such as the Oyewole brothers or Lawal for Economics.

It was 9:00 am when Musang got to the US embassy; there were people lined up already: a boy and two girls. He was happy to be coming from within Yaounde than from Bamenda directly as he had planned originally. He might not have made it to the embassy on time even with an early departure from Bamenda because of the numerous bribe-seeking police officers on the way who can delay a vehicle for as long as their corrupt whims dictate. Musang wondered the use of having so many police check points on one stretch of road or the other as if there was a state of emergency, yet all that these men and women in uniform do is slow down traffic by demanding ridiculous papers from drivers just so they could squeeze two or three hundred francs out of them. Sometimes these corrupt officers do not even ask for vehicle documents but expect the drivers just to give them a certain amount of money each time they go across a certain stretch of road as if that was the law. The officers target those drivers who try not to make these illegal contributions and delay them, wasting theirs and their passengers' time for no reason; yet, regrettably, there is no higher authority figure, it seems, to whom to file a complaint. Accordingly, travelling in Cameroon is like gambling: one can never tell when one will get to one's destination, unlike in other parts of the world where business partners could agree to meet at a neutral location out of town at a particular hour; not in Cameroon. A half-drunk police officer would hold one hostage for hours just because one has refused giving him a bribe. This is the case because the higher authorities in the force themselves get a fair share from what these so-called officers of the law collect from desperate drivers on the road. What an embarrassment that adult men, and women even, the supposed custodians of cultural values, bring home such filthy money to spend on their families, without any qualms.

Musang had just stepped into the embassy building and was still looking around lost and trying to figure out what his next move would be when a smartly dressed middle-age woman who was walking past suddenly stopped and questioned him.

"How can I help you, Sir?"

"Yes, I am here to apply for a visa."

"Okay then, you will have to bring out your passport, fill out one of those forms there and then go to that window over there with your documents. They will ask you to pay some money, your application fee, and then wait out there and they will call you for your interview. Of course, you have your supporting documents with you, right?"

"Yes, Madam, thanks."

"You're welcome," she answered as she walked away briskly.

Musang, still incredulous of the fact that the lady had addressed him as "Sir," which means he too was somebody important, did as was told and at the said window, he was asked to pay 10. 000 FRS as application fee. He was very disgruntled pulling out that amount of money for an application only. He thought of all the money he had spent trying to get a passport from his own country's government, and now he was upset the American embassy was asking him to pay so much in the name of a visa application fee.

"Musang! Musang Ngang Tijie!" called a man who, with a cup of coffee in his left hand, had just taken up place behind one of those thick glass windows from behind which questions are asked visa applicants.

"Sir!" answered Musang. "Those things must be bullet proof," he thought of the thick glass separating the interviewer from the interviewee as he approached the man who had called out his name.

He motioned Musang over with his left hand. "Can I see your passport?"

Musang dropped his brand new passport and the folder with his supporting documents into a drawer the man had pushed out from behind the glass under the counter top, and pulled it back after Musang sent in the document. However, the man picked up only his passport. Musang immediately felt stupid. The interviewer had asked for his passport and he had handed over everything he was holding. He hated himself for being nervous and wondered why at all he was being nervous. He made up his mind not to stupefy himself again; he would react to things as presented him and stop being nervous. Then he noticed the man had been scrutinizing his face as he looked at his passport.

"So you want to study in the US *ehn*?"

"Yes Sir," Musang answered.

"And for how long do you intend to be out there?"

"My program should last about four years and after that I will leave."

The man smiled sardonically as he spoke, with only his left jaw curving into a smile while the right side remained firm as if he had just suffered from a stroke: "All right then, come back after 2:30 pm for your visa."

"Thank you Sir," Musang answered as he turned and walked out of the embassy. "Is that it?" he wondered. He should be very happy given the stories he had heard about how virtually impossible it was to get a US visa, but he remained calm as he walked out, thinking of where to go and while time until it was 2:30 pm for him to return, pay for, and collect his visa. "These people are very strange," he thought to himself. "When least expected, they would question you until you would think you are on your way to heaven, then another person will show up and they would just give the visa as if a parent of his kept it waiting for him. 'Discretion,' they call it." It occurred to Musang to go to Melen neighbourhood where there usually are some Anglophones loitering for different reasons, the most obvious being the hope of running into an old friend and catching a free bottle of beer.

He would while time there, pick up his visa later on in the day and leave for Bamenda immediately, even if it meant arriving late at night.

It was 9:00 pm when Musang's bus, a fifteen-seater, glided down the Station hill into the valley town of Mankon, Bamenda. He smiled to himself as he looked at the countless light bulbs shimmering down below, his body relaxing into a strange state of wellbeing, which he always experiences upon returning to his village. His visa was in his left breast pocket; there was no parting with it. Tomorrow, Tuesday, he would go to Lengtieu, his friend working at the Post and Telecommunications, from whose office he would call Etonde, without any charges, to inform her that he had his visa.

Chapter 4

The morning was cold and promising a damp day. Ndzem sat on his veranda facing the Station hill from where thick rain clouds were already gathering as if to announce an impending rainfall. He had just returned from morning Mass and was sipping at his very hot cup of tea and biting into this long French bread sandwiched with fried eggs instead of his regular Calabar yam and bitter-leaf soup for breakfast. He always had this bread and egg breakfast on Saturdays as his way of remembering the short experience he had at his cousin's place in Yaounde when he visited about twenty years earlier. It was his first encounter with Francophone Cameroon where people are fond of quick meals of bread sandwiched with butter only, or margarine, and so on.

"'Morning, Father!"

"Good morning, Son. You must have rested well after that marathon trip to and from Yaounde."

"I am well rested, Father."

"In that case, sit down and tell me what is happening next. You know that where you are now in life, I have no clue of what is happening since I never went to Secondary school even. Now you people are talking of high school and even university. So what is happening next?"

"Well, there's still some time for me to take things slowly and put all in place before I can leave the country."

"That's so true, but what's there that you need to put in place. I would've thought you should leave now and spend all the free time you have out there getting used to the people and their ways before school begins?"

"That's true, Father, but since I begin in spring, which is sometime in January, and this is still September, there's more than enough time."

"Okay-o!" answered Ndzem laughing. "Spring! Why would a people name a season spring? It makes me think of a car or a bed instead—the springs—and then they also talk of fall. *Chei*!" Ndzem exclaimed before continuing, "These people, they sometimes complicate things. Instead of plain naming something the way it is, like "rainy" and "dry" season, they have to make it sound confusing. Spring, fall; I'm sure they have 'lie down' for another season?" Ndzem laughed aloud at his joke."

Just then, Mojoko approached the duo. "Pa Tsey," she called on Ndzem using the name of their fifth son who is also their youngest child, "there is something I would like us to talk about."

Musang stood up to leave.

"No, stay Son; let's hear what your mother has to say. Sit down Mojoko. What is it?"

"It is about this trip Musang is taking overseas."

"Yes, what about it?"

"No, nothing bad; I just wanted to point out to you that we have always asked our son to get married early on in his life, if he could. Now he is about leaving to go overseas and I am yet to hear you say anything about that to him."

"What do you want me to say? Am I the one to get a woman for him? Don't children these days claim to know everything? Why then should I bother getting a girl for him when he would only turn her down? I do not intend to bring that kind of pain to somebody's child, not me."

"I hear you, my husband, but we should not be frightened of our children because of what their friends have done to their own parents. You know, in a way it depends on how you bring up your children. You cannot take the taste of cocoyam and blame it on plantain. Even amongst cocoyams themselves you cannot do that: there is that which causes the throat to itch and there is that which does not, so how can you damn all cocoyams because of what one kind does to man?"

"Continue with all those your *panapo* and see if that is what will get a girl for your son."

Mojoko looked at her husband with a gentle smile on her face. "I came to talk to you, you have not even given me the chance to say what I want to say and now you are sounding as if I, Mojoko, refused you food."

Mojoko finally told Ndzem that their son was indeed thinking of intending a girl before his departure overseas. They both agreed it was a good idea because Musang would then be twice responsible, since he would always remember that he left a "tail" behind. He would be serious about whatever he was doing to return home quickly to his wife.

"As you know, Mojoko, I have never had a problem with our son getting engaged or married when he is financially stable enough to take care of a family? The drawback is where is the girl? Show me the girl and I will be on my way there to intend her for your son."

"Our son has found a girl he thinks he wants to marry!"

"What?" Ndzem questioned, surprised but excited. "Whose child is she?" asked Ndzem adjusting himself in his chair to be upright as he addresses the issue.

"I think you should be trying to know where she is from first before bothering about whose child she is."

"What are you talking about? What do you mean by where she is from?" asked Ndzem looking perplexed.

51

"I say that because she is not from around here."

"What do you mean by that? Where is she from?" asked Ndzem looking confused.

"She is my tribe's girl."

"She is your what?"

"My tribe's girl."

"So you think because I got married to a Bakweri girl my son should also get married in Bakweri land?"

"Hey, I did not go looking for a wife for your son. He can tell you how he got charmed by a Bakwerian. Like father like son, they say."

"I don't blame you," Ndzem retorted with a smirk.

"Why would you blame me? Is it not true?" Mojoko walked away laughing at her husband's surprise. "Talk to your son and see what plans he has; I have unfinished work in the house."

By the end of the day, Musang had his parents' permission to talk to Etonde about their intention to visit her family with a marriage proposal. Musang had not been this happy in a long time. He could already see Etonde as his wife. In fact, he would go to the US, rush his studies and return to his bride. Where could anything possibly go wrong with such a plan? The girl was his already, and like him, convinced they would have a bright future together. It was now for Musang and his parents to furnish her with the details of their trip; this far, Musang had informed her he would get back to her and he just did. He and his parents agreed he should do all that he needed to do within the next month before he left the country.

Musang and his parents arrived Victoria on a Friday evening, since Etonde had advised that her parents were always home on Saturdays. With her mother, they had informed her father, *Mola* Ngomba, of the arrival of her suitors on a Saturday a whole month away from when Mola Ngomba was informed. Upon arriving Victoria on the first Friday of October, Musang and his parents went to *Ni* Sama's house so that Musang should know the location of the house. *Ni* Sama was a family friend of theirs who used to work at the Delegation of Lands and Survey in Bamenda until they transferred him to Victoria. *Ni* Sama and his wife were very glad to receive them, especially because of the reason behind their trip. *Ni* Sama joked that if Musang, who is as a son to him, is already getting married, then it meant he must himself be an old man already. They all laughed and teased Ni Sama even more as they asked him if he thought time was standing still. It was about 6:00 pm when Musang left for Brandon's house, promising to be back first thing in the morning so together the family could get ready and leave for Sokolo. He was sure that with luck on his side, he would meet Brandon at home before he took off for his weekend drinking and nightclub dancing activities.

Ewune, Etonde's immediate younger sister, had hardly slept all Friday night as they prepared to receive Etonde's future in-laws the next day. Even then, she and her mother, Iya, woke up early to grate the cocoyam intended for the *timanambusa* with which to receive the guest. *Timanambusa*, about the core of Bakweri menu, is a local dish prepared from grated cocoyam on the one hand, and palm-kernel-oil sauce on the other. Measured scoops of the grated cocoyam are transferred into specially prepared plantain leaves, carefully folded, and then neatly displayed in a big enough pot, depending on the quantity being prepared. An appropriate quantity of water is added to the pot and boiled until it is done. Meanwhile, palm-kernel-oil sauce prepared with different spices, meat and dried fish is also being brought to a boil and left to simmer for a while so it thickens. When both the cocoyam paste and the palm-kernel-oil sauce are done cooking, the cocoyam paste, now looking like some kind of thick jelly-like substance, is sliced vertically into a number of chewable pieces, then the sauce is poured over it and stirred well so the pieces of boiled cocoyam paste are heavily drenched by the thick sauce. It is then ready to be eaten. The cook can also serve this dish with the sauce in a different bowl for the diner to do the mixing himself. However, the former with the mixture combined right in the kitchen by the cook and brought to the table like that is traditional and preferred by many. In fact, the locals hold that the name *timanambusa* comes from the traditional way of mixing these contents in a big bowl by repeatedly flipping everything into the air with a backward spin so the contents repeatedly and smoothly glide back into the bowl each time, and without any mess. This method is best at perfecting the mixing procedure. Preparing the dish is quite a process, hence the need for Ewune and her mother, Iya, to get out of bed a lot earlier than usual.

By mid-day, since Musang had promised he and his parents would show up around 1:00 pm, *Mola* Ngomba had taken his bath, changed into a favourite white long sleeve shirt and a thick loincloth, which he tied round his waist with the lower edge all the way on the ground. He sat in his parlour waiting while sipping palm wine from a glass mug locally called a "tumbler" or "drummata."

At exactly 1:00 pm, Ndzem and his family knocked on *Mola* Ngomba's door.

"Come in," answered *Mola* Ngomba, but the door was bolted from inside. "Who locked this door?" he bellowed at nobody in particular.

A boy of about ten, Ekema, emerged from the back door, which leads to the kitchen, running. He unbolted the door and stood agog with his mouth open as if he forgot saying what he intended to say because of the sight before him. He had never seen such a colourful outfit before in his life. Ndzem was in *'togɔ,* the distinguished traditional wear of the Ngemba and Grassfielders in general. It is usually sewn in black like a *boubou*, right to the calf or about the ankle of the owner. The attire has wide long arms that also go as far down as the full length of the outfit and it is marked by hand with colourful designs. Mojoko was dressed like the Bakweri woman that she is, in her traditional *caba ngondo*, a flowing gown, about five or seven inches longer than the woman dressed in it is tall, so she spends all the time picking up the gown from about her knee level so she does not step on it. The less formal version is usually shorter, more exact in measurements and so much more comfortable in terms of length.

The confusion on *Mola* Ngomba's face was obvious; more so, when he greeted and went on speaking Bakweri and Ndzem responded without the slightest non-native accent. "*Mola, nèh?* How're you?"

"*Iŋwe, owuri?*" As his Bakweri flowed flawlessly, Ndzem thanked his stars for all the years he spent growing up and working in Bakweri country—Bota, Bonjongo, Sasse, Bova, and other Buea neighbourhoods.

Mojoko joined Etonde's mother, Iya, in the kitchen leaving the men to chat for a while; they too talked their own women's language behind. When the girls were done transferring the food into the parlour, Etonde's family assembled: her three other beautiful sisters Ewune, Ngowo, and Endale, and her last and only brother Ekema, their father and their mother. On the other side of the parlour were Ndzem, Mojoko and Musang. *Mola* Ngomba spoke first.

"*Mola*, once more, you're welcome."

"God be praised," answered Ndzem

"So what brings you to our humble home?" questioned *Mola* Ngomba just to be formal as per tradition.

"That is a good question. A man does not bare his teeth for nothing; he must be trying to bite into something, at the very least, that is if he's not smiling. As you can see, *Mola*, your farm is very fertile, a sumptuous cocoa tree, he said referring to Iya, with so many ripe pods. I was walking past the other day, when I saw one of the pods. I was convinced it would taste very good, so I thought I should come and obtain your permission to harvest that particular pod."

"Iya, mother of our children, are you listening?" It was *Mola* Ngomba addressing his wife.

"I'm with you," answered Iya, with her eyes on her husband. "I think *Mola* here has spoken well and we get his drift. I am with you in whatever you decide, but let him identify the cocoa pod he is interested in, and then we can go on from there."

"Well spoken," answered *Mola* Ngomba. "Over to you *Mola*," he said addressing Ndzem.

"To show you that we're not strangers in this compound, and that we were formally directed to this yard, let me put this question to the floor since the family is here assembled. If anyone in here recognizes this visiting family sitting, please stand up and introduce us to your parents."

56

There was a slight hesitation, and then Etonde stood up, turned around and faced her father before blurting out in a slightly trembling voice, "Daddy, these are my guests. I met Musang through a friend at work and we have since grown fond of each other, until he told me he would like to spend the rest of his life with me. He pointed out that if I had no objection, then I should arrange for him and his parents to come see you and Mummy. His father is a Catholic catechist." Etonde added the last bit to let her father know they were a God-fearing family, something he had always asked them to take into consideration about anyone to whom they thought they could get married because, according to him, a God-fearing husband means peace in the household.

"And so what village are they from?" asked *Mola* Ngomba

"They're not from any village around here but all the way from Bamenda," answered Etonde.

"From where?" asked *Mola* Ngomba, the look on his face suddenly turning sour as he looked at Etonde and her mother with the look of a crouching tiger. "From Ba-me-nda?" He spoke emphasizing his words. "A Bamenda man to marry my daughter?"

"But his mother is from Bonjongo."

"Nye-nye-nye-nye-nye-nye," blabbered *Mola* Ngomba imitating the sounds of the words Etonde uttered last. "A girl like you, you want to get married, instead of getting me a Bakweri man from a wonderful Bakweri family, you go and bring me a *mojili* man for an in-law. Have you not heard of distinguished Bakweri families from where you could find a man? His father is a Catechist, what is he himself? Please clear out of my face." *Mola* Ngomba looked at his daughter as if he would kill her if he had his way. He stood up, picked up his walking stick, which is always leaning against the wall

57

behind the door and stepped out asking Ndzem to excuse him. Etonde ran out to the rear of the building crying. Her mother followed *Mola* Ngomba outside just as her siblings Ewune, Ngowo, and Endale, followed their sister into the back of the building, leaving Ndzem, Mojoko, Musang, and Ekema who appeared to be in a trance, all alone. Ekema was already admiring this good-looking man he had begun imagining would be his sister's husband.

Musang was equally confused, but Ndzem is the one who spoke up: "Poor girl, her father is one of those who do not want to see *Graffi* people. Our fluency in Bakweri must have fooled him until now. He must have been wondering why I was dressed like this." Just then, Iya stormed back into the house, apologizing for her husband's behaviour. She tried to get Ndzem and his family to eat but failed. Musang was past words; he just stared on at the blank wall across from him unable to believe the embarrassment. Just then, Ndzem stood up and so did Mojoko followed by Musang.

"I'm sorry this had to happen. I was thinking that if in my own days I could convince a Bakweri man to let me marry his late brother's only child and take her away to Bamenda, then this union could not be a problem this late in the day. A time has come when these fictitious differences imposed on our minds by vicious members of our society seeking private gains must stop influencing our lives. See how we're already passing it onto our children, and so forever siblings will continue fighting each other even as strangers cheat them of that which is rightfully theirs; whereas, together, they could've had a huge impact on the trend of events."

"*Mola*, like you have rightly said, this has nothing to do with Bakweri people as a whole; it is just that my husband has suffered in one way or the other in the hands of Bamenda people. He lost his position at work to a Bamenda man, and then he feels his oldest brother should have been one of the first Bishops in West Cameroon, but it went to a *Graffi* man. To make things worse, when one of our daughters was denied a position in Our Lady of Lourdes College, Mankon, he failed to see it was because of the competitive nature of the interview, with over a thousand students from all over the country vying for under a hundred positions. To my husband, it was *Graffi* people refusing to admit his daughter into Lourdes, even though he knew white reverend sisters were the ones running the school. So just like that, *Mola* has developed an aversion for Bamenda people, which is personal rather than cultural. After all, as you yourself have rightly pointed out, your wife is Bakweri and there are many Bakweri men around who are married to women from Bamenda. Go to all these CDC (Cameroon Development Corporation) camps and see all the mixed couples that are thriving there. Honestly, *Mola*, I had never foreseen anything like this else we would have dealt with it before today. Please give us time to talk to him."

"What can we say other than to express our sincere sadness at the fact that my brother would let his personal feelings destroy our children's happiness? Please excuse us to her and tell her we are sorry it came to this, but that she should rest assured she has earned our respect and love from all that Musang tells us about her, and that if we have to make this trip again, we would, so she should not be worried about our end. That said, I think we should be on our way then," Ndzem spoke with a weak and tasteless smile on his lips.

As if in a trance, Musang walked out with the carton containing the bottles of liqueur, which they had brought with them. It worked out well that they had not brought any palm wine yet. It was their plan to send for palm wine as soon as the talks were underway and things were going well since that is when they would have needed the palm wine to lace it with the liqueur and use it in blessing the marriage.

"Leave that behind son, you cannot bring it to his home and then take it away again. After all, who knows tomorrow? Even then, what is a carton of liqueur?" Ndzem spoke with the airs of a mature man who had experienced things in his life.

The group walked past the last junction, as far as the exit from *Mola* Ngomba's compound, close to the major road heading back into town, before Ndzem asked Iya not to mind going any farther, that they would find their way. He thanked Iya for everything and again assured her that they did not mind coming back should *Mola* Ngomba change his mind. They hailed a taxi for Gardens where *Ni* Sama's house was. Not a soul uttered a word during the ride as they all sat still stunned and unable to believe what had just transpired.

"*Iya-e-e-e-e!*" exclaimed Iya, a cry of despair, as she rushed back into her house clapping her hands and crashing on the floor as if someone had died. "Ngomba has killed me today," she wailed. Her children, but for Etonde, rushed into the house to find their mother in tears and wailing on the floor, "What would Ngomba not pass me through," she was crying and lamenting. That she called her husband directly by his name showed the degree of her anger and hurt. "What kind of disgrace is this, what kind of shame on my head, to agree for a people to come all the way from Bamenda for my daughter's hand only for Ngomba to bring shame on my family, *Tata-e-e-e-e*?" She wailed

"Mummy please take it easy and let it go," it was Ewune, herself in tears as she saw her mother crying.

60

"Let what go, Ewune? Let what go?" Her anger was not at her daughter but at her husband, yet she vented it on Ewune. "What kind of nonsense is this in this house? Your father would not respect these people all the way from Bamenda because he has his personal feelings about *Graffi* people? What kind of nonsense is this? If the origins of his daughter's suitor were that important to him, why did he not ask before agreeing that a suitor should come to see him for his daughter? What kind of shame is this on my head?" Iya was crying, blowing her nostrils into the edge of her loincloth and voicing her frustration at the same time. It was another occasion for her to recall all the nonsense she had taken from her husband for close to twenty years that they have been married. "This man thinks I do not have parents, else he would not dare treat me like this." When Iya finally got up from the floor, she went into her room, packed a bag for herself and left for her parents at Buea after instructing Ewune to take care of her younger siblings. Etonde herself still in tears dried her eyes, picked up her bag and informed her siblings that she was returning to her house in Mile 4 where she had moved out just within the last two weeks. She left without seeing her father. There was complete chaos at *Mola* Ngomba's residence laced with a pervading mournful air.

It was dusk when *Mola* Ngomba, tacking the road with his cane, approached his unusually dark and quiet house. "*We-e-i!*" He exclaimed as he called out for his wife repeatedly without an answer. "Iya, are you there? Iya, the wife of Ngomba, the son of Ngomba Wowoko from Wututu, are you there?" He always behaved like this, trying to sweet talk his wife when there was trouble, as if to remind her that she was married to a man of noble background. The silence rang on.

After another call, Endale, his fourth daughter, about twelve years of age, opened the door.

"Where is your mother?" asked *Mola* Ngomba.

Looking obviously angry herself and even daring to be spiteful, Endale blurted out without the characteristic affection in her voice, "I don't know; she left with a packed bag but did not tell anyone where she was going."

"A packed bag? What does that mean?"

Endale did not think it worthwhile answering, so she just stared on at her father. *Mola* Ngomba walked into his house and sat down, looking around for a while as if trying to identify landmarks to help him recognize his own home, then he asked for his meal. As if to remind him of his poor behaviour earlier on in the day, his daughters served him the meals intended for receiving Musang and his parents. After eating alone, which was uncharacteristic in his house, especially during the evening meals when everyone was usually present, back from work, school or play, he stood and went into his bedroom mumbling something to himself.

When Iya's parents saw her approaching and looking gloomy, they went into panic mode. "What is it this time? I thought the two of you had finally figured out what marriage is all about after all these years? Iya–*coco*, what is it this time?" Her father, *Mola* Njie, asked as he relieved her of her bag. Iya crashed on the floor as she started weeping again and telling her parents the disgrace her husband brought on her and the children earlier on in the day.

"*Tata-e-e-e*!" swore her mother, *Mbamba* Namondo. "No, that's not true. Did he not know they were coming?" she asked.

Iya only looked at her parents with narrowed eyelids and they understood.

"Then why would he do that? If where his potential in-laws were coming from mattered that much to him, then he should have posed that important question before giving his blessings for them to approach. Let him not do like this and bring bad luck to my granddaughters. " *Mbamba* Namondo protested.

"So you got angry and left?" *Mola* Njie asked with an implication that trivialized the seriousness of *Mola* Ngomba's behaviour, a kind of male or better still husband solidarity.

"What do you mean by that? Is that not very embarrassing?" asked *Mbamba* Namondo.

"But she should have waited and given it to him when he returned!" *Mola* Njie suggested.

"Leave my daughter alone. Is that how you do things? Is that how you do things?" *Mbamba* Namondo asked emphatically yet calmly. "Then why do you think she should take nonsense from Ngomba? Why would Ngomba not grow up even after all these years in marriage? Let him come here, I will tell him something just this once."

That same evening, Musang and his parents, completely frustrated, left for Bamenda with an overnight bus. As much as Ndzem spoke positively about Etonde but lamented what seemed to be the possible end of the relationship, he ended up telling his son to take it easy until they were sure they could do nothing more to bring Etonde's father to reason. He pointed out, however, that there would always be fish in the ocean. Musang did not say anything in reply. The mishap visited upon them by her father, along with the process of musing about Etonde and her wellbeing consumed him. He had known girls, but this was the first girl who had won his heart over completely. He could feel the flame burning in his chest, right there under his heart; it was as if he was going to die. He could not eat and barely spoke as he spent his time thinking of the implication of this rejection on *Mola* Ngomba's part. Everything had worked well on his side and he was sure he would be a married man before he took off for the US, only for this to befall him. What was he to do now? All of a sudden, he felt like seeing Etonde, yet he realized there was nothing he could do, nor had he anything new to say to her. "In fact, if any talking had to be done at this point, it had to come from Etonde and her family," Musang said to himself. Yet, with the way her father had behaved, it was obvious there was virtually no turning back on the father's part.

About two weeks had slowly gone by before Ndzem could find the courage to summon his family to sit and review the results of their trip to Victoria and its implications. After all, they wanted to hear from Musang what the situation was between him and Etonde given their encounter with her family and to concretize plans for his trip to the US.

"Father, I haven't spoken to Etonde since our return," Musang pointed out.

"Why?" asked Ndzem in disbelief. "You must be careful not to visit your frustration on the poor, young lady instead of her father. She didn't do anything wrong; it was her father."

"Even the poor mother was so upset we could all see it," added Mojoko.

"Please, do all to get in touch with her so we know what the situation is, and at the very least to console her. What kind of man do you think she would take you to be? You come this close to marrying a girl and then disaster strikes, which we hope is temporary, and you abandon her to herself? What kind of man does that?"

"Father, I don't think it matters anymore."

"What do you mean?"

"What her father did is a terrible thing; in fact, it's so serious I, personally, see it as an abomination. My parents and I cannot be humiliated in this manner and you expect me to want to be a part of that family still," Musang queried.

"That sounds responsible, but if you really love this girl, I think we should all be able to put our pride aside and move on with the arrangements whenever her father can reconcile himself to the situation. Insofar as I refuse to feel personally insulted by her father's unfortunate behaviour, I think, if you ask my opinion, you should not let a good girl like Etonde slide through your fingers. I did tell you there are many women out there, and that's true, but as long as there are chances of recapturing a run-away fish, continue casting. When I said there was enough fish in the ocean, it was only intended to help you deal with the pain you were experiencing on that day. There always will be women and men, true, but it is no easy task to find one with true love for you. I was watching Etonde all the time we were with her, the respect she showed us and the fact that she wanted us to have all we needed are remarkable qualities one does not find in the young women of your days. Young women these days spend time talking only about how beautiful and educated they are, yet they cannot boil a simple pot of rice for one to eat, as if one eats beauty and education without substance."

"I hear you, Father, but I am interpreting this differently: to me it is a sign, an answer to my prayers about my vocation in life. As much as I have been thinking about being educated and marrying a beautiful wife and having children, I have also been thinking about the priesthood, and my prayers were that the good Lord should give me a sign. I am seeing this as a sign that I am not meant to be married."

"What?" a startled Ndzem exclaimed in disbelief. Ndzem lowered his head into his left palm and repeatedly brought both his legs together and apart in such rapid succession that his whole body was shaking to the established vibration. Mojoko simply froze.

At last, Ndzem raised his head, looking grim and almost shocked. He asked, "Since when did you begin thinking like this?"

"I have been nursing these feeling for ever, even before I met Etonde, but things seem to be clearer to me now after her father's behaviour."

"In other words you have not rushed things?"

"No, Father, I have been thinking about this for long now. To me, this rejection is only a sign."

"And so what about your trip to America to study."

"It is my plan now to enter the major seminary; I will study there."

Mojoko was still in denial when she questioned her son. "What kind of study can you do at the major seminary other than being prepared for the priesthood?"

"Mummy, the major seminary is a part of a major university in its own right."

"Even though I do not have my own degree, during our days a high school certificate was alright just like a secondary school certificate worked wonders for the generation before ours. So what degrees do you come out of the major seminary with?" asked Ndzem.

"After one's study, one can have a degree in philosophy or theology for example. Even then, coming out of the seminary does not require one to go around looking for a job;

one becomes a priest upon passing out of the seminary," answered Musang.

"And should something go wrong and you can't become a priest what can you do with philosophy and theology?"

"What do you mean by something going wrong? What can go wrong?" asked Musang.

"*He-he-he!*" Ndzem laughed mockingly. "So you haven't heard of young men who spent years, four years even, in the major seminary only to be refused the chance to graduate and become priests for one reason or another? You haven't heard?"

"That is certainly extreme, Father, and in that situation, the seminarian must have done something seriously wrong."

"I hope so, because that's not what I am hearing from Christians these days; to them, becoming a priest is beginning to sound almost like another job in the public service."

"So what you are telling your father and me is that instead of going to America, you have made up your mind to stay back, go to the major seminary and come out as a priest?"

"Yes, Mother!"

"Hey! God almighty, what did I do to you? Musang! Musang! The thing that you will do to me in this family! Why don't you just get a gun and shoot me let me die and go? Why don't you just kill me?" she stood up crying and walking out of the parlour back into the open yard.

Ndzem did not say anything; he sat there with his head in both his palms, his thoughts racing. Even though he had once toyed with the idea of his son becoming a priest, those days were almost completely over, especially with the changes in the lifestyles of priests that he was beginning to notice. He had thought becoming a priest meant true devotion to the service of God through services to humankind and nothing else, so how is it that a triviality like tribalism, which ought to be beneath such a servant of God, is now thriving in church affairs instead? Father Alphonsus, for example, had never cared about who came from where when he was recruiting workers in the church, but now Father Kijung had to know where one came from before he could make up his mind whether or not to hire the labourer. As if this is not disturbing enough, a few days before, news of a priest from another parish who spent hours drinking in an off license shook the parish as parishioners vented their anger. Then there is that other new priest who dyes his hair and is quick to rush out of his cassock only to put on sumptuous African wears in which he drives around from one event to another socializing and looking like some local chief in the neighbourhood. Things like these have shaken Ndzem's faith in the future of the church on many occasions, especially when he thought of those days when one never knew priests had private clothes as they were seen in their cassocks all the time catering for God's sheep, their foremost concern. Here we are today with more priests who do not have to go on foot even, yet Mammy Nkah died last night without a priest to anoint her. There was a time even when he said he was still catechist just because of his faith in God and the good old Father Alphonsus who accepted him as catechist when he was sent up from Buea by Father Tilman in those good old days. Otherwise, he would have left and gone back into his community and engaged in trading and farming if not back to his coffee business. "This is not what it was when I was being trained in Bonjongo," Neighbours could hear Ndzem lamenting aloud from time to time: "After all, how many priests nowadays really care about the souls of their parishioners as once was the case? The administering of the sacraments—baptism, confession, visiting and anointing of the sick have all become work instead of sacraments that were being devoutly administered. In the past, priests saw these as different ways of not only winning souls for God but of serving Him directly and so snatched every opportunity to offer these sacraments, and they did it with such a devout disposition. " Ndzem thought of a few weeks back when a desperate Christian had asked a priest if he could listen to his confession only for the priest to refuse because it was not a day for confession designated by the local church's program. Yet, the priest had been chatting idly with some young men and women. His excuse was that he had to be somewhere else at that moment, even though he went on chatting for a few more minutes before finally walking to his car and driving off. Ndzem was only a catechist, but he knew, in any case, that these priests are trained to do all to attend to requests for the sacrament of reconciliation as it could mean the chance to save a soul for Christ. Father Tilman would have jumped to the opportunity and listened to the man's confession even in his car. As Ndzem contemplated Musang's decision, how strongly he felt that with the economy deteriorating as quickly as it was, one could use some extra help from a well-educated child in the secular world, only for his son to be talking of entering the seminary. Yet, he remembered how in the past he had prayed for, hoped for, and even encouraged Musang to consider priesthood. How was he now to take back his own words and still be a man in front of his son? He had shot himself in the foot and there was nothing he could do but go with the flow of things. There was nothing wrong with his son becoming a priest provided he would be a good priest or else he would deal with him himself.

"If this is what you now want in life, all I can do is stand behind you. The choice has to be yours, so that tomorrow you don't blame it on somebody else. You go and think about what you want us to do next, and we would do what we can."

When Musang walked out of his father's parlour, Ndzem clapped his hands in frustration. "The things the children of today would do to one. Today they want to be this; tomorrow they want to be that and so on. What is the use having children nowadays since they think they know better and will no longer follow advice given them by their elders, yet when they go out and get into trouble, they rush back to the parents they had ignored crying for help?"

When Musang left his parents that afternoon, he took a taxi directly to the Post and Telecommunications office to see his friend from whose desk he usually made free long distance calls. Lengtieu was in. He called Victoria with the intention of talking to Etonde but decided to talk to Brandon first; they talked for over twenty minutes. It was heart wrenching to hear how much Etonde had changed in the way she related to people in general, men especially. According to Brandon, Etonde barely greeted her colleagues anymore and she ate alone at a different location instead of where they used to eat as a group. She rarely smiled and no longer went to nightclubs. Brandon confessed how difficult it has been for him to bring Etonde back to her old self. She simply says the old Etonde is in mourning and cannot socialize anymore; that she would stay that way until Musang will return into her life.

After listening to what Brandon had to say, Musang could not bring himself to talk to Etonde, so he decided to go through his friend. "*L'homme*, do me this favour: tell Etonde I am sorry for what happened, and that I wish I could turn back the hands of time. Tell her that although I have loved and will always love her, I have taken what happened as a sign that I am not to get married, and so I have decided to go into the seminary for that which was my first and only love until I met her. "

"You have decided to do what?"

"You heard me. Please deliver the message for me. Thanks, and I will stay in touch."

In disbelief, Brandon listened to the dial tone for a while before slowly returning the receiver to the hook.

Chapter 5

It was a Friday evening when Musang and fourteen others of his class arrived Mambuyi to begin a new school year at the campus of St. Xavier's Major Seminary. Mambuyi, where the seminary is situated, is a remote and appropriately quiet village setting up in the distant hills on the way to Kom, somewhat a neighbouring town, at least nominally, to Mankon and Nkwen. From the campus, one can see the road to Kom meandering on through the undulating grassy landscape of the region. A number of priests and advanced seminarians who were walking around for this purpose, pointed out to the new seminarians the way to their hostels before giving them guidelines on how things were to unfold from then onwards. They immediately went to church for Mass to begin the new school year, then to the cafeteria for their first meal as aspirants to the priesthood. Inside him, Musang felt a sense of relief and satisfaction that he had at last found his vocation. Thoughts of Etonde flickered in and out of his mind from time to time, but he was sure it was just because he was human and that with time all would be over; he would forget her and she would forget him. All he now had to do was focus on a life of prayer and penitence. He would pray for himself, his family, and all his friends, so their souls can go to heaven someday.

Time passed, and as the days, weeks, months, and years came and went, the students got busy with a rather rigid program from one stage to another: it was Mass, classes, meals, prayer and then private studies all day long. Occasionally, they entertained themselves playing soccer, but that was as far as it went; they were not a part of the local schools and universities system as such, and so the seminarians did not participate in the College and University Students' games known by the French acronym OSUCS. They studied to become priests; that was it. A rather tough curfew that limited the seminarians' ability to go in and out of town for whatever reason made the solitary nature of their lives on campus more intensive. Their lives were under the watchful eyes of the school's authorities and even the parishioners where they served from time to time: a single negative report could mean the end of one's years as a seminarian. Once in a month, the authorities gave the seminarians time, about half a day, to go out and visit family and friends within the surrounding towns and villages. At other times, depending on how advanced the students were in the program, there were opportunities for them to go out and serve in different parishes within the archdiocese for a period of time that gave them some first-hand experience of what being a priest is all about.

It was during one of such periods in his life as a seminarian that Musang, then in the third year of philosophy, received a surprise visit from his friend in Victoria. Brandon had come to Bamenda to visit his own parents whom he had not seen for years. Musang was at the Bayele parish, a neighbouring town to Mankon, and he was indeed a popular seminarian. Brandon had found out about Musang's presence at Bayele from his own mother who belonged to the same Bayele parish. It was after the 10:00 am Mass on a Sunday when Brandon approached Musang who was still in the sacristy in the process of disrobing. Musang turned and saw Brandon standing at the entrance into the sacristy; they both smiled at the same time, Musang for not having seen his dear friend for such a long time, and Brandon in disbelief at the change his friend had undergone physically and even in his mien. To Brandon, Musang's crew cut was completely out of place on the head of the character he had known Musang to be, and then he saw his friend in a pair of leather slippers looking calm, humble, and composed, the portrait of a true religious: one who had denied the outside world so to say.

"*L'homme*," Musang called out gently as he walked up to his friend.

It was a relief to Brandon his friend still called him by their mutual nickname, *L'homme*, unlike some friends who become religious and think it means denying who they used to be as simple, ordinary, secular human beings. Yes, they had to deny their sinful past but not go around uptight and unable to joke as before as if becoming a religious is a punishment of some sort. Brandon found that in spite of the different changes he could clearly detect in his friend, his sense of humour was still there, but he talked only about decent topics and nothing about girls like they used to do.

"*L'homme*," Brandon answered back to his friend, "how're you doing?"

"I'm doing great, hardly anything to complain about."

With a strange smile on his face like one in pain but trying to hide the feeling, Brandon blurted out: "*L'homme* you surprise me, not that I didn't know you to have a religious side, Man, but priesthood?"

"That's life, full of surprises," answered Musang smiling calmly. "I succeeded in surprising myself too *L'homme*. You know how much I loved Etonde, but when her father would not let his daughter marry me because I'm *Graffi*, it shattered me and made me believe my vocation was different from the call to a marital life. Nobody knows exactly how I loved that

75

girl, for which reason I couldn't see myself married to another girl with Etonde still alive."

"Now that you've mentioned it, let me tell you that you destroyed one of the most beautiful and equally sophisticated girls I've ever known, Man."

"What do you mean by destroy? That's really harsh. It was her father who destroyed us."

"I'm blaming you because you didn't give her the support she needed from you when she needed you the most."

"What do you mean? What could I've done?"

"What could you have done? What could you have done? You could, at the very least, have been by her side and helped her heal before you took this all self-righteous decision of becoming a priest." Brandon was suddenly angry like Musang had not seen in a very long time, then he suddenly calmed down, breathing deeply to relax. "*L'homme*," he went on, "for days Etonde called in sick, and then when after two weeks she showed up for work, she looked like a ghost—pale and without her usual make-up and zeal for life. As soon as she saw me, she broke down crying and I had to take her into the back to help her calm down and keep everyone from seeing this queen in tears. Then she quickly told me what had happened and can you imagine how I felt that you and your parents left town without you even thinking you could tell me, let alone Etonde?"

"*L'homme*, I'm sorry, Man. I know I should've done all to tell you, but the pain was going to kill me. How was I to face you? How could I take in Victoria again knowing that Etonde was around yet we had nothing to do anymore, or that that was what her father wanted?"

"But *L'homme*, we are brothers, Man, what makes you think I would not have understood what you were going through? I know I do not love with the conviction I saw in your love for Etonde, but I have had my own heartbroken too, so I could have been able to relate to your pain."

"I'm really sorry, Man, I'm sorry, but that was the best thing I thought I could do at the time to alleviate my pain. I'm sorry. I can now see how selfish it was; I'm sorry"

"I hear you, but please don't do that kind of stupid thing again. By now, you should have known that I'm someone to whom you can talk. I may not have your disciplined life style, but I think I know you well to understand when you are hurting. I might as well tell you that Etonde has not changed ever since this happened years ago. It's as if life came to a standstill for this girl, Man. She can now manage a smile, but that's all. I try to be by her as often as possible and I think she is beginning to trust me. She says as stupid as it sounds, she can't bring herself to love let alone marry another man. She said she'd wait for you."

"What? You mean after all these years she is still talking like that"

"Yes! She doesn't go out to clubs like we used to do when you met us, but stays home all day when she isn't at work. From time to time, she returns my visits and each time that happens, it is you we end up talking about most of the time. She says she would consider the battle lost only when you are ordained; until then, she knows you are her man, because she knows how much you loved each other."

"That's true, but now things have changed. I have chosen a different route in life. *L'homme*, do your man one favour?"

"And what's that?"

"Please do not let Etonde wait for me; I am almost a deacon now; the meaning is that I am more likely than not, to become a priest. Why would she waste her time waiting for the impossible?"

"What do you want me to say or do? All I can tell you is how I saw this girl suffer for you. She cried for days; that was when I knew she couldn't be left alone. By the way, she has moved from that house in Mile 4 where she was just before you came down for the "knock-door." She is now living close to me, and because I thought it was too much for her to be alone while going through all this, I convinced her sister, Ngowo, to move in with her just so she could have somebody to talk to when in pain. Between then and now, she has turned down two marital offers from successful men from equally rich families in this town, I mean Victoria. Since the day you people left, I was made to understand she didn't visit their compound for a whole year. She went there only when summoned by her father, and I hear on such occasions, when she got there, she would not talk to him. She would talk to her mother and her siblings that was it. See the madness you brought into a man's daughter's head?"

"Don't blame me, *L'homme*. If I could see into the future, I may not have bothered trying to know her since I would have known her father would stand in the way. I am really sorry, but it's all too late now. In any case," as his eyes welled and his heart burned in his chest, Musang tried to change the topic of discussion, "so how is Maggie doing?"

"Maggie left me, and she is currently somewhere in France. She couldn't stand my friends and my temper. According to her, of all my friends, you're the only true friend. She is convinced the rest were there just to drink and help me squander my money."

"I'm sorry to hear that, and I'm also sorry I can't now bring you to the priests' house. It is almost time for lunch and we must be together; you know your man is still just a student."

"No, no, don't worry, I understand. I just had to see you for myself even if only to believe all the news we were getting in Victoria. Moreover, I know Etonde wouldn't forgive me if I returned to Victoria without seeing you. She didn't send you any message, but I know better; she loves you dearly and is still in a lot of pain. I'm sorry I'm saying this to a man in your position, but what else can I do?"

"All I can say is how sorry I am."

"Stay well and take care, Man. I hope becoming a priest would not mean you can't visit us?"

Musang smiled gently as he waived his friend goodbye. "Just pray for me to become the priest first. It is not as easy as it may seem, and, of course, priests do visit friends and family from time to time. Take care *L'homme*, and thanks for everything." Musang spoke as he walked away.

Brandon stood still and looked at his friend as he walked away in his white cassock until he entered the priests' lodge. It was like a dream to him. Indeed Musang was the friend of his whom he respected the most, for as lively as he was, like the rest of them, he was principled. He respected the girls he dated and drank very little, if at all, but Brandon had never thought of his friend as a priest. For a brief second, his eyes welled as he watched his friend retire. Life suddenly seemed empty to him without Musang, the one true friend besides their mutual friend Wesley whom he could call at any time for them to discuss virtually anything. The problem was, with Wesley almost everything was like a big joke, and it took him quite a while to sense the gravity of a topic, whereas Musang was always on cue. Musang could tell when a joke was no longer funny or when a story was not meant to provoke laughter, as funny or as ridiculous as it may be.

On his part, as Musang walked away, he was also swarmed by feelings of nostalgia for the good days of old when he used to spend time with his dear friend in Victoria and they would go around like free bees alighting on every flower that caught their fancy. "Not so any more, not so…," he thought to himself as he twisted the doorknob to the right, opened the door and disappeared within.

When finally the time for Musang to return to the seminary came, he had remained a popular seminarian in Bayele parish. Everybody loved the quiet, hardworking, and always smiling seminarian. He had time for everyone who tried talking to him and as always, a word of advice. Like the Psalmist, he always told Christians, "Always fear the Lord, for that's how you know you are wise." Even the rector was very happy with the letters he received about Musang and his time in Bayele. It was with determination and conviction, therefore that Musang settled in to face three more years as a seminarian, but these would be years of theology, philosophy just having been completed.

Seminary life is rigorous, especially in Mambuyi, but as the years came and went, Musang became even more convinced of his calling: he was to become God's priest and win over souls to God almighty. And so at their ages, although they felt more like convicts with strict curfew hours and only a visiting Sunday each month during which anyone could visit them, or vice versa, those whose call it was to be priests someday, felt at home—they ate, worked, studied, and prayed.

The rhythm of his life was steady and uneventful until at last Musang was in his sixth year as a seminarian, in Theology III in other words. The meaning of this was that he was now far advanced as a seminarian. He was beyond being a lector who could read in church, or an acolyte who could serve while a priest celebrated the Holy Mass. Musang was already a deacon, the dream position of every seminarian as it meant only a year is left, and in most cases a few months only, before ordination into the Holy Priesthood. In fact, when the occasion presented itself, Musang now assisted priests on the altar during Holy Mass: he fills the chalice with water and wine for the priest, helps raise the chalice during consecration while the priest raises the Sacred Host, helps in distributing Holy Communion, and after communion, cleans the Sacred vessels. Accordingly, Musang did all to prepare himself for his vocation: he spent long hours in prayers, remained humble and full of respect for authority, and whenever possible served at daily Mass. His parents were very proud of him as Ndzem dreamed of the day of his ordination. He was already planning with relatives what their role in the ordination would be like, the gifts they would get him and so on.

It was the sudden death of Rev. Father Tony Tilman that took most of the priests and major seminarians to Buea for his Requiem Mass and burial. Given the long years Father Tilman had served in Buea, the town was full to capacity with guests. Musang could not be away from the burial of the priest who gave him his first holy communion, whose altar boy he was for years. The bond between them was just too strong. It was Father Tilman who trained his father as a catechist and had him serve in Buea until he advised him to move to Bamenda and join Father Alphonsus who needed a trusted and devoted catechist. In Bamenda, he would be closer to his own people and so could begin preparing for his retirement with a lot more ease, when the time came, than if he were in Buea. Even Ndzem romanced the idea of attending the funeral but for the expenses such a trip would entail. It was equally to cut down on his expenses that Musang concluded he had no choice but to put up at Brandon's house in Victoria. Even if he had wanted to stay in a hotel, not only would it have been too expensive for a poor seminarian, the two main hotels in Buea—Mountain Hotel and Hotel Memoz—were already full to capacity.

As happy as Brandon was to see his friend, he found himself in a rather awkward situation. Musang was not only completely transformed and with this aura of spirituality about him, he did not know what subjects to broach with him, so generally he had to wait for Musang to initiate topics and then he would fill him in.

"So *L'homme*, how is Bamenda and Mambuyi in particular?" Brandon ventured.

With a faint smile on his face as he reacted to the name "*L'homme*" after such a long time, Musang responded, "We are there trying to survive. Bamenda town though, is expanding rapidly. Foncha Street has been bulldozed and we hear there are plans to tar it very soon. Ndamukong Street is also being graded now as we speak. So, you can imagine how quickly the town is growing. In fact, Cow and Ghana Streets have already been tarred."

"So you came to bury a priest?"

"Yes! How did you know?"

"It has been the talk of the week with virtually every Catholic man and woman planning on attending the funeral Mass. He must have been a very important priest then, else he would not pull such a crowd of lay people and the religious alike from all over the country?"

"In a way, but 'important' is not the word here. Virtually everyone is important; I think it has to do with the services he rendered to his community, and, again, he was about the last of the Mill Hill missionaries we had serving us. I am not even sure if he was Mill Hill, but one of those foreign white priests serving us. Remember great names like Bishop Rogan, Bishop Julius Peeters and the rest? This priest would fall into that category although he never became a bishop. He served all the villages around here and trained many in the fear of the Lord. He was the lone standing priest in Buea for years before local priests began joining the priesthood. It is for that reason that he is really well known, respected, and loved by the people."

Brandon registered the changes his friend had undergone; even his attention to the exact meanings of words caught him off guard. "So without the death of this priest, you would not be here?"

"We are brothers *L'homme*. When my ordination is over, I would, from time to time, have some vacation time and then I would be able to visit you more often."

Brandon smiled to himself and bowed down his head. That was not what he meant; it was not what he was trying to ask Musang, but he did not know how else to frame his question. What he was trying to find out was if really all was over between Musang and Etonde. To Musang, that was history, but not to Brandon and certainly not to Etonde who continued rejecting suitors and is wasting her time, according to Musang, talking about waiting for him. Musang could tell Brandon had something on his mind.

"*L'homme*, what is it you are trying to tell, ask, or find out from me?"

"I am sorry about this, Man, and I hate coming across as a tempter in your life, but do you know Etonde is still the same even after all these years?"

Tears suddenly welled into Musang's eyes just as he turned and stared into the street below through the only window in Brandon's parlour facing the back, which, ironically, is the main approach to the building. His mind went to times when he had leaned against Etonde's body at that very spot as they both looked out at the scene down below. It was also the spot where he used to stand and stare in expectation of Etonde's arrival. "I am sorry to hear about that. All I can do is pray for her. I loved her, but I am a different man now *L'homme*, I am a different man now," he whispered those last words. "How nature toys with us and fashions us into whatever we are destined to be. I will pray for her to understand." Musang was thinking about these invisible yet concrete lines or boundaries in the lives of human beings, which more often than not, cause so much pain. Without such boundaries, he would be part of a happy couple today with one of the most distinguished young women he had ever known, but he was from the wrong part of the country according to her father. If these lines were not drawn by region, it would be tribe; if not tribe, it would be class; if not class, race and so on, instead of people just trying to live happily together as children of God. He wondered at this seemingly superficial, yet sometimes concrete animosity between the people of the coast and those of the hinterland, brothers under the English, and one people during the colonial era, and he just could not fathom how they let this happen to them. He remembered a group of young students

84

from both parts of the country discussing it and agreeing it was a government strategy designed to keep an otherwise powerful people apart while those in power, strangers alike, mismanaged and squandered their resources.

Brandon's question brought Musang back to more immediate issues: "So what's your program like?"

Musang started out of his thoughts. "Yes, we get done with Father Tilman's burial today Saturday, but I cannot travel on a Sunday, so tomorrow I will go to Mass here, spend the rest of the day with you and then leave on Monday."

"That's fine. Today being Saturday, we now work, but it is only half day—until 12:00 noon—so we should be together in the evening when you return. See you then."

They both walked out of the house, Brandon on his way to work and Musang to the Bus Station to pick up a vehicle for Buea. Brandon continued shaking his head in disbelief at the transformation his friend had undergone. Musang had on a Roman Collar, with a black suit that fitted him well, as usual, and a black leather folder containing some papers and prayer books. A small black bag in which he had his cassock dangled from his left shoulder as he walked on. He now walked with an erect gait and his stare on the ground in front of him, unlike in the past when they, as young men, swaggered with their heads in the air taking in the scenes and people, yes, the girls.

The Cathedral in Small Soppo, Buea, was packed beyond capacity, with the crowd overflowing onto the well-trimmed surrounding lawns. Musang was surprised to see women crying as if it was a close family member who had died, instead of a well-known and loved priest. In any case, he understood; he himself loved Father Tilman so much although he could not bring tears to his eyes. It was a long service that lasted more than two hours thirty minutes. In the end, Father Tilman was buried outside at the head or altar direction of the Cathedral. Musang chose not to go to the reception that followed. In his white cassock and Roman Collar, some people were already addressing him "Father," taking him for an ordained priest. He answered quietly as he walked past, relishing the title; after all it did no one any harm, and he was just several months away from his ordination. It was wonderful to find himself amongst so many priests from all over the South West and North West parts of the Cameroons especially, and he blended in as one of them.

In a room in one of the buildings that they had been shown upon arrival as a temporary rest house for priests during the occasion, Musang took off his cassock, folded and returned it into his bag. In a sink in an adjacent toilet, he washed his hands and wiped his face several times with his wet hands as a way of cooling down and removing some of the excess oil on his face, thanks to the sun. He walked back into the neighbouring room, picked up his belongings and stepped out into the surrounding grounds where people were already vying with vehicles for a way out of the overcrowded premises. He hoped to get onto the main road leading north to Buea Town and south to Victoria through Saxenhof and Bonjongo subsequently. Taxis were not common in this area, but with luck, he could find one that would take him directly southwards to Victoria or northwards to Bongo Square on the main road leaving Buea. From there, he would easily find a vehicle for Victoria. Musang was still lost in his thoughts trying to figure out where to position himself by the roadside when he heard a voice: "Which way are you going, Father?"

"I'm trying to get to Victoria," he answered.

"That's where we are headed. If you don't mind, you can ride with us."

"That would be wonderful; thank you so much," Musang answered as he approached the vehicle.

The driver pushed open the back door from inside and Musang sank in just as his mind established the fact that it was a Catholic couple on their way back home from the funeral.

"Thank you so much."

"For nothing," the driver answered. "I'm Doctor Ojong and this is my wife, Julia."

"Hello Madame," Musang greeted. "My name is Musang, and I'm with the Major Seminary in Mambuyi."

"Wonderful! You mean you came all the way from Bamenda for the funeral?"

"Yes, many of us did. In fact, there're priests from all over the country, I gather."

"I am not exactly surprised. Father Tilman was a great man and trained many of us at some point in our lives. He was the true apostle who never tired of checking on his flock."

"That's so true," Musang confirmed.

"I was an elementary school pupil when he was parish priest in Buea Town. In fact, we transported the blocks that were used in building that church to the construction site, I mean St. Anthony's Church Buea Town," Doctor Ojong observed.

"That was a remarkable contribution to the church."

"That's true, Father. You know, in those days Christians had a lot more commitment to the church than today, it would seem to me." The conversation went on and on with

Doctor Ojong speeding along the narrow road with so many blind corners: the nearby grass had invaded the road at virtually every possible spot, transforming even harmless curves into dangerously blind corners.

It was 6:00pm, and still day, when Musang slammed shut Doctor Ojong's car door at the junction from Gardens just as the doctor was about turning right to drive towards Bota. "Thanks for the ride, and God's blessings to you and your family."

"Thank you, Father, and have a safe trip back to Bamenda." Doctor Ojong zoomed off with those last words.

"*L'homme*, you are back!" It was more of a statement from Brandon as Musang stepped on the veranda.

"I'm back."

"I hope it went well."

"Yes, it did. The crowd was huge and one met people one hasn't seen for ages."

"Okay, you may be surprised to learn that I still haven't started cooking in this house. In any case, I placed an order to the woman who cooks for our bank on special occasions and she has prepared something for you to eat. You will find the food in the kitchen; I am going out as usual. You know I've only the weekend to relax and have fun. I'll see you in the morning. "

"Just take care of yourself."

Brandon giggled as he stepped out into the darkness outside. Musang undressed, changed into his pyjamas, ate and then spent the evening reading his bible. When he noticed he was beginning to read some lines more than once, he knew it was time to go to sleep. He put his bible by the bed, knelt down and said his night prayers before climbing into bed. His mind started playing back things he and Brandon had done in that same room earlier on in life, to the point where Etonde's image flashed across his mind. He could not run away from it; she was all over the room, even her gentle laughter could be heard echoing in the night air as he struggled to fall asleep. He was thinking of Etonde and their times together when he was overwhelmed by a strange sense of calm; he fell asleep.

After Musang returned from church the next morning, he ate his breakfast and sat listening to songs by his favourite musicians: Ekambi Brilliant, Manu Dibango, James Brown, Burning Spear, and others from the Congo. Brandon who had returned at about 4:00 am was still sound asleep. Musang was thinking of nothing in particular as the songs soothed his spirit when there was a gentle rap on the door.

"It was about time," Musang thought, thinking about the woman who was supposed to have brought his lunch by mid-day although it was already 1:00pm. Without his mind on what he was doing, he pulled back the door expecting to grab a basket. He pulled back more confused than surprised. "Etonde!" he spluttered.

Etonde stood looking at him and did not say a word. They stood like that for some seconds, which felt like minutes, and then regaining his composure, Musang urged her, "Please come in, come in," he said stepping to one side. Just then, the woman with the food swung into view from one end of the building so Musang just held the door open until she got to him. "I can take that," he said going for the basket. "We were expecting you a long time ago."

"I am really sorry; our priest took too long for Mass today, two hours which was spent scolding Christians for not contributing enough, nothing else, and so by the time I got home I was already late. I am really sorry."

"That's okay, thanks."

"Thank you too," she said as she withdrew.

Musang turned to see Etonde still standing behind him as if confused. "Please sit down."

"Where is Brandon?" she asked gently with that soft coarse voice with its strange soothing effect to the entire body. "Could you please let him know I am here?" Her voice was calm as always.

Musang went into the bedroom and Brandon emerged rubbing his eyes. "Etonde!" he called out as a way of greeting.

"You this pagan man. If it is to the nightclub you would go, but not to church."

"I always try to make the evening Mass at 5:00pm okay. Why are you standing up as if you are a stranger? Please sit down."

"I just stopped by thinking Cynthia would be here so as to invite both of you to the house for lunch. It is obvious she is not and you are still sleeping, so I will just go back home. Whenever you are ready, you can come over and eat some *timanambusa*, which I prepared."

"Etonde, please sit down. As you can see, I have a guest. Musang came in late on Friday and since then I have not been able to make time to see you. I stopped by yesterday before going out to Miramar with Cynthia but you were not at home."

"I was two rooms down playing monopoly with my neighbour, the girl who works at BICIC. I'm sorry nobody heard anything." Etonde was looking pale and seemingly running short of breath. "I am sorry, but I must go."

"Etonde, please sit down. I haven't seen you for a long time now." Musang could not recognize his own voice; it sounded stifled and hoarse.

"I have always been there if you had wanted to see me. And of course, you are not here to see me, so why bother?"

"Etonde, even if it is fate that has arranged this, should we not talk for a while before you leave?"

"Talk, Musang? Talk? Talk about what?" Her lips parted in what looked like a smile, but she fooled nobody. The pent up feelings of pain and hurt were welling. "Talk about the fact that you left me stranded in love? That you pretended you cared about me when you never really did? Musang, what do you want to talk about?" Her voice was no longer calm as her entire body trembled from the power of her overwhelmingly painful emotions.

"I always did love you Etonde."

Etonde giggled before she spoke, "Musang please stop, you never did, or else you don't know what love is. You thought you loved me but you never did. To think of the fact that you even wanted us to be married," she smiled as she moved her head from side to side, then she took in a deep breath and exhaled slowly.

Musang was standing by her, holding her hand and gently pushing her into a chair. She dropped into it without saying a word. "Etonde, I always did love you and I know what I am talking about."

"Only for you to run away because of a small problem caused by my father? Yes, I know it was a terrible thing my father did, but is that how you would have abandoned me in the face of the slightest challenge we might have had as a couple? You saw me fighting my father, with my mother by me, and instead of standing by me you left me to fight alone, and then as if I was responsible you never called back to check on me knowing how heartbroken I was, Musang?" Tears rolled down Etonde's cheeks as she sniffed. "You

91

refused coming to talk to me on the phone even after I took the initiative and placed a call to your friend's office and scheduled a moment to talk to you, you would not come? I pestered Brandon here until… but what could the poor man tell me? What could he tell me, Musang?" The dam caved in and Etonde cried with a rare abandonment of her emotions that let loose the pain she had welled in for years, wailing and moaning in a hushed manner. Musang moved over to her seat, took her in his arms and held her tightly as if to give some rein to her trembling as her body convulsed in her anguish. Musang held on until she started regaining control of herself, and when she was finally quiet, he dared a few words of apology.

"Etonde, I am so sorry. I take every blame. I was too embarrassed to think right. "

"Embarrassed? Embarrassed for how long?" She spoke as she dried her eyes. "You even went away from the scene of your so-called embarrassment, whereas I had to continue facing the scene and the people who knew I was about to be traditionally married. My un-dying love for you transformed me almost into a widow even though you were still alive, but you were just too proud to come and look for and why not even claim the woman you came so close to marrying, and yet you continue talking about love? Please do not use that word again; you certainly do not know its meaning. I am sure about that. I wish you well as a priest." Etonde stood up and stepped out without even talking to Brandon who had quietly withdrawn into his room leaving the couple in the parlour. Musang rushed into the room after Etonde left.

"*L'homme*, who told her I was here?"

"What do you mean by that? Didn't you hear her explaining why she had come? Or do you think we no longer

92

talk to each other? No, we do. In fact, we became great friends after all that she had to go through because I was there for her. I was her support, and but for the respect I have for you, I would have considered dating her. That would have been very cheap of me though because it would have amounted to taking advantage of a girl at her weakest moment in life, which is wrong. Secondly, she could never stop thinking and talking about you; she hasn't either. Like I told you, she said she would stop on the day you are ordained a priest."

Musang stumbled out into the parlour, crashed into a chair, leaned back, shut his eyes, inhaled deeply before exhaling long and hard.

Musang, who had fallen asleep, came around slowly as he familiarized himself with his environment. He looked at his watch, sighed and stretched; it was already 4:00pm. Brandon was standing by waiting for him to become fully awake. "I am going to Etonde's house to eat my *timanambusa*. Why don't you come along? If nothing else, I think it would be a nice opportunity for you to apologize again, without her being so much upset to figure out what you are saying, for all the pain you've passed her through."

"The pain I passed her through?"

"But you heard her, and why is it so hard for you to get; she said it herself even if you would not accept it from me. After her father's blunder, if you had been there for her she would have won the fight against her father, but he used the fact that you went away the way you did to argue that you were not serious about the marriage in the first place."

Musang's head dropped in acknowledgment of his error. "Indeed, I owe her an apology. I think my pride controlled my handling of the situation instead of my love for her."

"I think so too, and I always said it to you but you would not hear anything from me at the time."

It was a ten to fifteen-minute walk to Etonde's house; they walked along taking in the streets and the people milling about. As they stepped onto Etonde's veranda, which Brandon had pointed out from a distance, Musang unconsciously fell back. Brandon knocked on the door and waited. He heard the bolts pulled back and the door creaked open gently. Brandon stepped in and the door blind fell back in place blocking Musang from view.

"You bolt your door during the day like this? What are you afraid of?"

"It's just a habit I developed as a child growing up. My father always locked his doors or at least had them shut." Etonde was trying to shut the door when she felt the pressure from outside. She pulled back the blind to find out what was happening

"Good evening," greeted Musang. "Can I come in?"

Etonde could not find her voice, so she stood still just looking at Musang who walked in and shut the door. It was obvious Etonde, though calm as usual, did not know what to do. She sat down in the closest chair as if to keep herself from crumbling to the floor.

"*L'homme* sit down," Brandon urged. "Etonde where is my *kwa-coco*?"

The question brought Etonde back to the present. She smiled as always. "You have just come in and all you want is your *kwa-coco*. You can't even greet nor are you interested in finding out how I am doing," she joked.

"I will greet after my stomach is full, and I can always find out how you are doing anytime," he spoke laughing.

Etonde moved about and in a few minutes food was on the table. It was Brandon who invited Musang to the table. It felt like a blade through his heart.

"I will dish and sit down here. It is more comfortable down here than up there. You know I have never liked dining chairs and their heights." It was Musang and to nobody in particular.

When they were done eating, they sat drinking and chatting, but it was only Etonde and Brandon talking. Musang was quiet. When at last Etonde and Brandon seemed to have exhausted every possible thing they could talk about, Musang cleared his voice.

"Etonde, I came over here because I wanted us to talk, especially with what happened earlier on today."

Etonde looked at him and smiled gently as if to say what is there you could possibly want to tell me now after all these years.

"I know and can taste the bitterness in your smile, but after all what I have seen and heard from Brandon who remains a dear friend to both of us, I thought it would be nice for me to come and have a chat with you."

Etonde sat still, staring at him. Brandon was about excusing himself to walk out when Musang stopped him: "Stay *L'homme*, please stay; there's nothing about Etonde and me that you do not know, and I would like you to continue being in the picture as you have been these past years." He turned his attention to Etonde. "My dear Etonde, where can I begin? Where indeed can I begin? What can I say at this point even that would matter, especially with all what you have been through because of me? It is for that reason that I just will not refresh your pain by going over certain things again. I have realized the mistakes I made, alas how late am I. I was selfish and saw only how I had been embarrassed, and in my error bundled your family into one unit that had humiliated me; it did not even occur to me that you felt twice humiliated and was fighting against your father for me. If it is any consolation, how I wish I had seen things differently, the way I see them now. It is in this light that I dared stop by here today, wondering if you would even let me into your house, just so I could tell you how sorry I am for having hurt you so much. True to your very sweet nature, which endears you to all of us, you've still let me into your house. What a lesson in tolerance and forgiveness you teach me sweet and gentle Etonde. Being away in Bamenda could have made it a lot easier for me to deal with the situation, comparatively speaking, and in view of all what Brandon kept telling me, but coming back here, seeing you and hearing you talk, has given me a whole different picture of what *we* and not *I* went through." Musang emphasized the pronouns. "If you can find it in your heart to forgive me that would be wonderful; otherwise, I will forever, after today, pray that I may someday hear those kind words of forgiveness from you, Etonde." Musang paused after sounding her name and looked into her eyes, before finishing off his statement, "I am truly sorry."

Etonde remained calm and kept looking at Musang even after he had stopped speaking as if his words were causing her to replay something on her mind. Then she smiled gently as she started into the present by jerking her head backwards in a quick move, at the same time holding back tears. "Musang," she whispered, "I could never stand in your path because I did not bring you to me; you came to me and I don't know how, nor can I say why. Both of us have heard it said if something is yours it will always come back to you. Maybe I suffered the way I did because you were my first, as you know, in spite of the environment around which I grew up and the nonsense I saw happening before my own very eyes for years. If you ask me why I went against my principles when I saw you, I cannot give you an answer, yet the truth is that there was something about you that was different; something that gave me the feeling of wholesomeness whenever I was around you and heard you talk. It was as if something had been missing in my life until I saw you and heard your voice. But then, that is all of no consequence now. If it means anything to you, then let me say I forgive you, I had forgiven you else I might not have been able to live on even. I can't say 'move on,' because I have always carried you with me. I pray for the day that I will be able to break away from you. I say this not to make you feel guilty or what, but just because it is the truth. I forgive you Musang, I forgive you, and I wish you every success." Tears glided down Etonde's face as she spoke those last words. Musang was confused for a second or so but then regained himself and, for the second time in one day, moved over and joined Etonde in her chair and held her to himself just as Brandon stepped out of the room into the open night air. She cried and sobbed heavily for about a minute or two and then as if ordered by a voice she alone heard, she stopped and dried her eyes.

"Musang, I think you should go now."

"I was about saying that," Musang replied.

When they both stood up, she hugged and held him tightly for a brief while, brought her lips onto his lightly for a quick kiss and then pulled back and opened the door. "Bye!" she whispered.

"Bye!" answered Musang squeezing her hand before breaking the grip.

"Etonde, see you tomorrow," said Brandon as a way of bidding goodbye.

"Yes, you will," answered Etonde as she withdrew into her house.

Musang and Brandon walked about five minutes without talking to each other. "I'm sorry it came to this."

"No, it's alright," answered Musang "in spite of all the pain and tears. I think it helped bring a kind of closure to both of us, and so I hope we can both move on now without the other. Is life not a wonderful thing? Look at this incredibly beautiful and well-mannered girl with men dying for her, yet she will not give in because her heart is still with a man she loved years ago and who is not even still in the picture."

"No, you may have thought you were no longer in the picture but to her you are the picture; you have been the picture until today, hopefully. I sincerely wish she has been able to break free of you today or at least will be able to find the power to do so after today because I have seen this girl suffer since she lost you. You know, *L'homme*, as we were growing up, I always heard that women love differently from men, I have seen it from this your thing with Etonde."

"I still do not agree with that though. I think men also love genuinely, but it has to be the right time and the right person. I think when both aspects collide the love is bound to blossom."

"I'm not going to argue with you. All I am saying is that now I believe there is and can be true love between a man and a woman, and it is different from just wanting to go to bed with the other."

"I think we both agree there." Musang spoke as he entered the parlour after Brandon. He slammed the door shut

98

and bolted it. You know I leave early tomorrow. When I wake up, you will still be asleep and I will not want to disturb you especially as you have work in the morning. Please do me one favour -"

"And what is that?"

"Promise to let me know, always, how Etonde is doing until she finds a different man."

"That's not a problem."

"Thanks, *L'homme*; thanks for everything."

"That's okay, Man, that's what true friends are for? Don't make me get emotional. You are just becoming a priest and not dying. We would still be together, right?"

"Sure, why not. You don't seem to believe me when I tell you that priesthood will not tear us apart. All right then, go to sleep. I will do same after my night prayers."

It was 4:30 am when Musang woke up. He wondered if it was the rain that woke him up or his body clock, which he had, through practice, learned how to program it to wake him up whenever he wanted to be up. He took his bath, got dressed, grabbed his bag and small traveller's umbrella, unfolded the umbrella and snapped it open as he stepped out into the early morning darkness. He deliberately refused going into the room for fear of disturbing Brandon who slept lightly. As he walked past the direction to Etonde's house, his heart swelled with mixed emotions—sadness, affection, nostalgia—but he moved on, striding purposefully even as he thought of Etonde in bed alone. "This Victoria with this its rain," he mumbled to himself, "I was wondering if I would come and go without it raining." Musang was the last passenger to fill up a fourteen-sitter bus.

Just before the bus was about to take off, the young man who had loaded the bus drove it to nearby Shell Petrol station and was filling up the tank when the real driver showed up. The young man then stepped out of the driver's seat declaring: "Okay, you all should travel well and safe. This is your real driver."

Surprised by the switch, a woman from behind asked, "So what are you?"

Everybody laughed as he ran away excited about the amount of money he had received from the driver as compensation for having filled the bus with passengers. It was the practice that while the driver supposed to embark on the long journey is resting, a different person, an acquaintance of the driver's, is busy filling the bus with passengers for a token financial gesture.

"Good morning!" The driver greeted as he looked around the inside of the bus as if to make sure the number of passengers was what he was told he had. He saw Musang in his Roman collar in the awkward seat by the door behind intended for children or a driver's aide. "Morning, Father."

"Good morning," replied Musang.

'Father, please come in front here," instructed the driver.

"There is somebody there, I thought."

"Yes, there is one police man going to Tiko, but we have to pick him up at Mile 4. He will sit there. After all, he is going only to Tiko, which is not that far away. We always leave one seat open for *rammassage*, Father, which sometimes brings in a lot more money than if the seat was covered by a passenger going straight to Bamenda," the driver spoke referring to the practice of picking up and dropping off passengers from one destination to another nearby location along their drive to Bamenda.

"Well, thank you then."

"Thank you, Father. I am sure you came to bury that Father who died," asked the driver as he shifted the bus into gear and veered it towards Mile 4 on their way out of Victoria. It was an interesting enough topic on which to begin their six to seven-hour drive back to Bamenda.

Chapter 6

Three weeks had gone by since Musang returned from the burial of the late Father Tony Tilman when Father Foinjem, the rector of the seminary, summoned him to his office one Tuesday afternoon after lunch. The rector informed him that a meeting had been scheduled for him to meet with members of the Vocations Board in three days, which would be Friday. The rector would not tell him what it was all about, but he knew from past events that with something of this nature, it meant his progress as a potential priest was in some kind of trouble. Not being guilty of anything, Musang was sure this was something he would easily resolve, so all he had to do was wait patiently while praying about it.

It was exactly 9:00am on Friday when Musang, neatly dressed in his white cassock and Roman Collar, like the deacon he was, with his breviary in his left hand, knocked and walked into the rector's office. He was shown to the waiting area in front of what they, seminarians, know to be the room in which the fate of many an ex-seminarian was decided. After about fifteen minutes, Musang was ushered into the room by Father Foinjem, where he saw four other priests, two of whom, like Father Foinjem, were core faculty members, with terminal degrees in Canon law—Father Wufei, and Father Kijung his spiritual director; he had never seen the other two priests before. For the first time since the rector told him of this meeting, fear seized Musang, in spite of his conviction that he had done nothing wrong.

"Good morning Deacon," greeted Father Kijung first, then Father Wufei followed.

"Good morning, Father, good morning," Musang replied after each priest's greeting.

"Please could we stand up and pray for the guidance of the Holy Spirit before our deliberations?" It was Father Kijung who spoke.

Two hours had gone by when Musang stepped out of the rectory and walked towards his hostel with his gaze on the ground. Other seminarians were looking furtively from different locations: rooms in the hostels, classrooms, the shades of trees where some like to sit and read their bibles and so on. They all knew the meaning of such summons and very rarely did a seminarian return from there smiling. It was Deacon Wirban, a mate and close friend of Musang's who joined him midway from the rectory to walk with him back to his room; a kind of moral support seminarians always give their fellow brothers "in trouble" as they say.

"So what is all this about Deacon?" asked Wirban.

"My brother, I am completely speechless. To cut a long story short, they claim they have noticed a slackening in the spirit of devotion that usually characterized my dealings in matters of my vocation, the church, and our faith ever since I returned from the burial of Father Tony Tilman. They asked me to confess if there was something on my mind. I did confess, brother, of an encounter, which to me helped instead in bringing about closure to a pre-seminary experience I had about six years ago. I told them the whole story of my experience with this girl and how we resolved everything when I stumbled on her during my visit to the South West. According to Father Wufei, it is a major blessing that this came up, and so I should try to resolve it instead of running away by hiding behind a cassock. I assured them I was not running away from anything, and that this is something that had been resolved six years ago and if at all anyone still had issues with it, it was the girl and not me, but they would not buy it. Father Kijung was categorical that I go on probation. However, when I told them that that was a waste of time since I was convinced I had resolved the issue and no amount of years on probation was likely to bring a different result, they asked me to step out and give them a few minutes to deliberate, which I did. It took these men only fifteen minutes, fifteen minutes to decide my fate, Wirban? They gave me the option to go on probation or try another vocation. I was not allowed to say anything after they gave me their decision, and as if joking Father Kijung tried convincing me that a married life is equally venerable in the eyes of God and society. This man sounded as if that was something I was hearing for the first time, some mystical knowledge, which I did not have before joining the major seminary, knowledge which had to wait for him to give me on this special occasion, the sixth year of my stay in the seminary, the threshold into priesthood, a life for which I have worked so hard. I had to quickly step out of there before I said or did something I would have regretted all my life."

"Musang, I am really sorry to hear this. I wish one could do something about it. You being sent on probation? Do these men know what they are doing? Why is it I am getting the feeling that only the very best seem to be thrown out of the seminary while most of us not in the slightest way worthy of this vocation get ordained? If you, of all people should be sent away from the seminary, especially after all these years, then what kind of men are they looking for to transform into priests? Why don't they listen to the side of the deacon each time they get to this point?" Wirban was talking to himself as he paced about in Musang's room. Wirban suddenly looked tired and years older than his real age, and had Musang not known how much they loved and cared about each other, he would have thought Wirban was afraid for himself instead of having been traumatized by his friend's predicament.

"Wirban, if it were for me alone, I can deal with this thing, but what will I do with my mother, my father? When my life crashed the first time when I tried getting married, it almost killed them. Then they found solace in the idea that I was becoming a priest and they were convinced it was something I really wanted to do, now this? Will this not kill my parents? What kind of humiliation is this? These men just toy with our lives because they were themselves chanced to be ordained? Do they know the kind of pain they are inflicting on families by decisions taken in such a seemingly nonchalant manner even while calling for boys to venture into the seminary because the church needs more priests? We make these sacrifices and enter the seminary with a burning passion to serve the Lord, only for men who are hardly better than we are to throw us out without apparently thinking of and weighing the consequences? Was it not Father Beri who told us just a few months ago after his studies in the United States that once someone made it to the major seminary there, he was sure to graduate as a priest?"

"Yes, unless he himself chose otherwise instead of the system throwing him out as is the case here with us," added Wirban.

"Why is it that we copy things from the West but must always give them an African twist, which seems always to be vicious? What is wrong with our people? There they call the head of a primary school 'principal,' by the time it got to Africa it was 'headmaster;' there a medical doctor is down to earth, friendly, and explains what he is doing to his patients, here our doctors are arrogant gods and virtually abusive of their patients; there they have transparent democracy, by the time it got to Africa people would kill you for belonging to a different political party, especially if it is not the one they consider popular with the masses. Beyond that even, our politicians will never give up office graciously. One idiot will cling to power for life and would not hesitate killing his own people if that was what it would take to keep him in office. What really is wrong with us?"

"So what's happening next?" asked Deacon Wirban in denial.

In a calm voice that belied the storm of confusion raging in him, Musang answered, "They gave me until tomorrow Saturday to leave on probation to Njimafor parish or until Sunday to vacate the premises."

"So why don't you go on probation?"

"Go on probation? Go on probation for what, Wirban? Have you not been listening to me?"

"But -"

"But what? Don't we know sending one on probation is just the beginning of a long drawn out drama that will, without doubt, end in one being sent home finally? Tell me we do not all know this pattern after all the years we have spent on this campus with these men? Why do you think I will be an exception given the number of seminarians we have been through ever since you and I came to this campus as seminarians? Why will Musang be any different? If I believed deep down in my own heart that it could lead to my ordination if I went on probation this time, you know I will go. But I am sure you know better, especially as I have nobody up there to stand for me, so why delay my pain and waste many more of my years? We are not growing any younger you know." It was when he stopped to look at Deacon Wirban in his eyes that he realized that he had been packing his things even without being aware of it or conscious of his surroundings.

"Why are you weeping Wirban? Why are you crying? Please don't make me cry. I need you to be strong for me." Musang stopped what he was doing and walked up to Deacon Wirban and put his right hand on his left shoulder in consolation.

"I am sorry, and a very troubled man," said Wirban drying his eyes. "If people like you are sent out of this place, then I am worried about the kind of life I will have as a priest."

"The Lord will take care. You know what we always say: *'Cow way yi no get tail?'*"

"*Na God di drive am fly,*" they both concluded.

Musang went on speaking, "You must remember that we always said we wanted to become priests so as to serve God through our services to mankind. Keep that before you at all times brother. With that as your beacon, I am positive you will make the good priest I see in you dear friend. If you also remember that we had come to the realization that priests are also just men, then you will never be surprised by another priest. Let God be everything to you Wirban, and like your favourite model, Padre Pio, no matter what decisions shall come up against you, remain always humble and obedient that you may always soar in the eyes of He who matters— Yahweh!"

"Thanks Brother, let me let you do what you are doing." Wirban walked out of Musang's room into the corridor outside where about four other senior seminarians were waiting quietly. He delivered the blow.

It was Sunday morning. Musang, in ordinary clothes, attended Mass with the rest of the seminarians, all of whom were already aware of his predicament and understood that since he had taken the Sunday option, it meant he had decided to quit. After Mass, as many seminarians as could find the chance stopped by in his now vacant room to wish Musang well. Deacon Wirban and two others helped him carry out his belongings, which consisted of two suitcases containing his clothes and some cartons with his books. Virtually everyone who saw the group leaving the hostel towards the direction of the main entrance into their campus stopped and wished him well, or from a distance waved goodbye to their once-upon-a-time fellow seminarian. This was the most unwelcoming sight to every seminarian as it was a reminder to every one of his own potential fate until he had been ordained a priest.

The group with Musang's belongings stopped at the main entrance into the seminary by the main road leading into Nkwen and then Mankon, a spot from which they were sure he would easily get a taxi. They had been waiting for about an hour when Father Kijung drove out of the seminary onto the main road and off to town as if he did not see them. The seminarians, along with Musang, exchanged glances but said nothing; the gesture was self-explicit: he was already of little or no consequence to the system and structure he had just left behind. With that display from Father Kijung, Musang, immediately, realized how difficult the road ahead of him would be, yet deep down in his heart he trusted in God. From his father's guidance and six years in the major seminary through all kinds of pain and challenges, he had built a relationship with his heavenly Father that he refused to let ordinary human beings dampen. "God is good; it is mankind that is always trying to ruin His plans," he spoke out loudly to himself. He was convinced nothing happens for nothing, and like his late friend Mufor was fond of saying, only God writes straight between crooked lines.

After about an hour and thirty minutes at the entrance into the seminary, they finally got a taxi. Wirban, with the help of the taxi driver, loaded Musang's stuff into the trunk of the car, the other junior seminarians having returned to school after they saw the look in Father Kijung's eyes as he drove past. Musang sank into the front seat after hugging his dear friend and waved goodbye to him as the taxi sped off to town. How differently the environment looked and felt as he explored old sites he had been seeing on a daily basis but this time with the notion that he was uncertain of that which was likely to make him come this way ever again. He was now looking at the seminary surroundings as an outsider. Musang sat with his eyes closed for most of the roughly twenty minutes' drive into town; the driver thought he was sleeping and that was fine with him. After all, what would the driver understand if he had started a narrative about the tragic nature of his life hitherto, a life that takes off with so much promise each time, only to crash with equal momentum?

When Musang got out of the taxi at the Nkwen Motor Park, he left his belongings in a pile in the middle of the Park and went into the closest wine and beer off License where he sat down and asked for a bottle of *Beaufort* beer. He emptied the first glass in one swig and then refilled his second, which he held and was staring in front of him at nothing in particular. He was glad nobody was around who recognized him as the deacon who used to be at Bayele Catholic Church. Slowly, Musang emptied his bottle of *Beaufort* and was surprised at himself: it was the first bottle of beer he had ever emptied in his entire life. His favourite drink was Top Citron and when he really wanted to socialize then he came up with a strange blend: half a glass of any beer and the other half of Sprite. His friends laughed at him when he did that, but that was Musang; he just did not drink beer.

Ndzem was walking back home from doctrine classes where he had been teaching aspiring first holy communicants the doctrine of the faith, as usual, when he saw his children crowded at the door into his parlour. His heart skipped a bit as he feared for his brother who had been sick all this while and they were just doing all they could and praying for a miracle for him to recover. Accordingly, Ndzem was already trotting by the time he got to his threshold to find out what the matter was, and then he saw Musang sitting in one corner.

"Mojoko, what is the matter? What is going on, and why did someone not come call for me?"

"You wanted me to send for you that what? What was I to tell you?"

"So what is the matter?" asked Ndzem on the verge of losing his temper.

"Musang has killed me-o-o-o, Musang has killed me!"

"Musang, what is your mother talking about? By the way, why are you people crowded here? Haven't you seen a woman crying before? Go back to your chores," ordered Ndzem threateningly. As the little group, which now included some of his neighbours' children dispersed, Ndzem turned and faced his son, "So what is going on."

"I have been sent away from the seminary." Musang did not mince his words.

"What? You have been what? For what? Why? What did you do wrong? Hey! Sh-sh-sh-sh!" Ndzem turned and hushed his wife. "Yes? That you did what?"

"Father, when I returned from the South West where I went for Father Tilman's burial, about three weeks after, I was called to the rector's office and given a three days' notice for a meeting with the Vocations Board. When I met with them, five priests, some of whom you know—Father Foinjem, Father Wufei and Father Kijung—claimed to have noticed that I had changed in the way I was relating to my vocation and that it seemed my mind was still concerned with secular instead of spiritual matters. They ordered me to confess the truth, and I did. I told them of my encounter with Etonde whom I happened to have met briefly, and by accident, when I was in Victoria and spent the night at my friend Brandon's place and she happened to stop by. We talked very briefly about the past and I apologized for all the trouble I had caused her. That was it and I left and returned. For this reason, I was being asked to go on probation because they felt my mind was still to be completely free from secular affairs, by which they mean thoughts of marriage. All efforts to assure them that I was fine met with deaf ears. From experience, Father, when these people start sending you on probation, your chances of being ordained are as good as zero. How can I know that and accept to go on probation? Because that was the ultimatum, they gave me: go on probation or consider myself no longer a seminarian. I decided to leave."

"So that is all what you did for them to give you an ultimatum? They did not catch you in bed with this girl or something of the sort?"

112

"No, Father, nothing like that. How could I jeopardize six full years of my life like that?"

Ndzem stood up as if in a trance, his nostrils flaring with rage, and walked out of the house without a word to anyone. As he walked up the road towards the church, he was talking to himself. "After all my years of service to the church, this is the pay they give me? My son, for no reason, is kicked out of the seminary? What do these people want from me? Why is life treating me like this? Father, God, why? Why? Why are you doing this to me? Why Father? Why is it that everything my son goes for leads to disaster instead, even after I call your name on a daily basis for these children? What Father, what do you want me to do?" Without knowing it, Ndzem had wept and was drying his eyes as he approached the Bishop's house. He did not know what he was going up there to do, but that was the first thing that came to his mind since he could not easily get to Mambuyi to ask the three priests who had dismissed his son what exactly they thought they were doing. After all, the Bishop is the head of the church and so the rector has to be under him.

When Ndzem walked into the Bishop's house, a mansion perched on a knoll overseeing part of Mankon town, they were just about closing the doors for the day, but knowing him to be the catechist, the Reverend Sister in charge let him in.

"Sister Nyuybe, can I see the bishop?" asked Ndzem.

"But you know it is past business hours, Catechist?" the sister pointed out.

"I know Sister, but this is not about business; this is a personal matter."

"I am sorry, but I haven't even seen the bishop all day, so I don't even know why I didn't say that in the first place."

"I have to see the bishop, Sister, I have to see him. Can you imagine that after all these donkey years serving the church, this is the pay they give me? They send my son away from the major seminary during his final year? Six years gone like that? Can you imagine that? After six full years? They are sending him out now that he should do what? Six years? Is that how the church repays its own servants?" Realizing he would not be able to see the bishop, Ndzem turned and walked out. He was determined to tell the bishop his mind when next they met. "They must understand that they are dealing with human beings and not pass people and their children through such hell with such nonchalance. Do they know what it is like to bring up a child? Do they know?" Ndzem was speaking aloud and angrily but at no one in particular as he stormed back down towards the direction of his house. He was still talking to himself and raging on almost past Mojoko without seeing his wife but for the fact that she called out.

"Father!" Mojoko called out to Ndzem the way the children address him. She does this whenever she is being affectionate. "Where are you coming from?"

"Where am I coming from?" Ndzem repeated after her. He was still very angry and raised his voice without knowing it. "Where am I coming from? After all the years of my life that I have given to the church, and they send my child away from the seminary after six years? Six years, Mojoko? I went to look for the bishop so he could tell me why my son has been sent away from the major seminary."

"Father, please take it easy, please come home and eat something first. You have not eaten all day. You left in the morning that you would be brief in the mission only for you to stay there until doctrine classes and then on your way back

114

to meet with this. You have not eaten and this is not good for your health. Please, remember what you always told me? That when the good Lord closes a door here He opens a window for you there? I was bitter myself my husband, but let us remember that God works in mysterious ways. Let us not be angry, especially as this child says he did not do anything wrong. Please, let us not be angry; instead, we should offer everything up to God in prayers. He alone knows what His plans are, so please take it easy. Please, take it easy." Mojoko sent her hand and held her husband at the wrist, like a little child, and led him home. Ndzem had been held spellbound by Mojoko's words and the affection they carried. She knows her husband can get angry sometimes and so she is always quick to go bring him back home before he does something crazy, like when he almost became physical with a new and young priest who disrespected him by calling his name without any traditional epithet of respect. He was angry because this was a child he, virtually, brought up and trained in the faith. He watched him go through school and as soon as he was ordained priest he thought he had become something else and was haughty towards and dismissive of virtually everybody who came his way. Had Mojoko not shown up on time, nobody knows what Ndzem would have done to the young priest.

Ndzem barely ate, and then went off to bed without even his evening prayers. Mojoko who could not remember the last time her husband had gone to bed without commending his family to God almighty to whom he always gives thanks for life and the family with which He had blessed them watched and followed him closely. She was determined not to leave him alone. Mojoko quickly noticed Ndzem was tossing in bed and even talking in his sleep; something she had never noticed before. She woke him up and led them in their night prayers before hugging her husband whom she reassured that they may not be rich but they have been abundantly blessed, and it is not this time that the Father in whom they believe so much would abandon them. She stopped talking when she heard the rhythm of Ndzem's breathing; he had fallen asleep.

When the next morning Mojoko got out of bed, she saw her husband already in the parlour rocking himself in his favourite chair.

"Morning, Father."

"Morning, Mother," he greeted in return. "I hope you slept well."

"I fell asleep after all."

"I'm sorry for all the trouble I caused you."

"You don't have to apologize, I understand. You don't even look like you have rested at all."

"Tell me how one can rest when things keep going wrong in a child's life like this?"

"I understand, but you must accept things as they come. By the way, are you not going for Mass this morning?"

Ndzem did not say a word as he turned and looked in a different direction.

Alarmed after she saw the look Ndzem gave her from the side of his eyes in response to her question, indicative of the fact that he was not going to church, Mojoko queried, "Who will arrange Father's things before Mass? *Tata-e-e-e-eh!*" She cried.

Ndzem sat as if he did not hear Mojoko. From experience, Mojoko knew not to push him when he behaved in this manner, and so all she could do was watch in silence even as she prayed for her husband to calm down.

Weeks had come and gone when one fine day, upon returning from morning Mass Ndzem, whose ways were slowly returning to normal, sat in his parlour and asked Mojoko, the rest of the children having left for school, to call for Musang who had gone to tether the handful of goats he owns to graze.

A few minutes went past then Musang showed up, "Father, you called?"

"Yes. Please sit down, let's talk a little."

Musang, with expectation, sat on the edge of the chair directly facing his father with his eyes on the floor in respectful submission.

Ndzem cleared his throat before speaking. "One month has gone by since you came home, which convinces me that indeed that's the end of your aspiration towards the priesthood. So what next?"

"I've been going around dropping off applications for a teaching position with these Catholic Schools like Sacred Heart, Lourdes, St. Bede's and so on, with the hopes that I could be given a teaching position in one of them. There are so many schools around and so I am hoping it won't be a problem."

"And that would be it? No plans of going further with your education?"

"Right now I'm looking at the short term, Father. If I can get something to be managing with, then I can come up with a better long term plan."

"I see. I just wanted to be sure of what you were planning. It's hard for me to be seeing you like this on a daily basis without knowing what you're planning."

"I understand, Father."

"Okay, thank you."

Musang stepped out leaving his father staring into one of the walls with an expressionless face.

Very slowly and almost inconspicuously, time passed as month after month came and went. Musang's hope of finding a job with the Catholic mission had failed. All the principals, priests he knew in person, claimed not to have any opening that fitted his qualifications. The Catholic Education Secretary, meanwhile, just kept avoiding him. "So what's the point with all these degrees if I cannot even use my knowledge of philosophy or theology to teach," wondered Musang aloud. His hope that the church could give him a temporary position to teach even religion in one of the Catholic schools around went dead.

By the start of the second year without a job, even Musang's clothes which were once new and e*n vogue* were now mostly threadbare. His appearance no longer mattered to him. He usually suffered from headaches, but he was determined not to let people know he was suffering, even though his appearance spoke louder than any words he could have uttered. It was his friend at the seminary, now Father Wirban, who used to come down, occasionally, from his parish in Akum, to visit with him and would leave him a little money, from time to time, which he virtually hoarded for rainy days. Musang was determined not to inform Brandon of his predicament for fear it would get to Etonde, but the way things were going, he had no choice; he needed all the help he could get from anywhere. Accordingly, he decided to get in touch with Brandon.

It was a Monday morning at about 10:00am, when Musang decided he had to make a call to Brandon. His friend, Lengtieu, at the telephone exchange who always helped him make such calls free of charge, was now avoiding him. At least that was the impression he had after trying to get in touch with him on several occasions only to be told Lengtieu was not in; whereas, he had seen him entering his office from a distance. Had this happened only once, the story of his not being around might have been considered the truth, but three times, even when he had seen him from a distance? Musang was convinced Lengtieu was now avoiding him. May be he had become a nuisance to his friend, especially without he himself seeming to have any future whatsoever. Accordingly, with some of the money Father Wirban gave him, Musang decided to pay at a phone booth to get across to Brandon.

"Hello!" came a voice from the other end. It was Brandon's.

"Hey, *L'homme!*"

"Hey, *L'homme,*" Brandon called with familiarity dawning in voice. "So how are things, Man? Long time!"

"*L'homme,* things are not going, Man. I have kept quiet all this while because I was trying not to burden you with issues."

"*L'homme,* what's going on?" asked Brandon with so much concern in his voice.

"*L'homme,* I'm just fed up with life, Man, so much so that I'm even beginning to think I may be cursed."

"What are you talking about? What's going on?"

"It's over a year today since I left the seminary."

"What do you mean by 'left'?"

"I could have said 'dismissed from the seminary,' but that would not be true. I was, for a strange, if not ridiculous reason, given the option to go on probation or leave the Major seminary. I chose to leave instead."

"Wh-a-a-at? *L'homme,* how could you keep a thing like this from me, and for so long?"

119

"I didn't intend to, Man. I thought I should first try dealing with the situation, and then when things calmed down a little and I was somewhere doing something, I'd let you in on it. But the way things are going, I'm likely to lose my mind at this pace. Things are tough. I'm living with my old man, and thank God for that, but can you imagine that your man goes for weeks without even a single one hundred francs coin on him? I have only one priest here with whom I was in the seminary who bothers about how I am doing, the rest behave as if I'm now something to be avoided; I mean even those with whom I was in the same class in the seminary."

"Man, I am sorry to hear this."

"Yes, *L'homme*, many pretend to be friends because the going is good. It's when things are tough as they are now that you know your real friends."

"Why don't you come down and be with me instead of bothering your old man. Again, a change of environment will really help you recover."

"That would have been a fantastic idea given that I am fed up with the way people look at me around here now. It's obvious almost everyone, but the members of my family, is now considering me a failure, yet I know deep down in my heart that this is not the end. I would have loved to join you Man, but I can't do that with Etonde still there."

"Yes, she is here and still not dating, so what are you going to do?"

"*L'homme*, I don't want her to see me like this, Man, no way."

"So what are we going to do? I think you should be able to take things as they are and face the world that way."

"That's easier said than done, my brother, I'm telling you the truth. I alone know what I have experienced, within this last year, particularly, in the hands of people I would have considered family even, given how close we used to be, especially when I was in the seminary. How they have all just changed, slowly but surely."

"But you know, *L'homme* that even in the case of opportunities, there are more out here than in Bamenda. Out here, if it is not in Victoria, it could be Buea, Kumba, and it could be in Douala or even Yaounde. Bamenda, in a way, is cut off."

"That's true but—I don't know, Man. I will see. I just wanted you to know my situation."

"Thanks for letting me know. While you think about joining me down here, I will keep you informed of any opportunities that come up. We may even just have to try so you leave for the US. Anyway, when we meet we would discuss this opportunity. So many of our friends without half your qualifications are leaving for the US, so why not you who are so well educated?"

"Thanks, Man, thanks."

"By the way, there is a Mr. Takang in Cam Bank Bamenda, please after about an hour go to him and tell him I sent you; he should give you some little thing to put in your pocket."

"Thanks, *L'homme*, and God bless you."

"Call me, *L'homme*, call me should things be a little too rough for you to handle. I don't have much, but I think the little I have can help us until you find something doing."

"Thanks, Man, and remember not to let Etonde know anything about my situation."

"No, why? Bye now."

Musang stepped out of the telephone booth with a feeling of elation he had not felt in a long, long time; it was as if someone had lifted a huge weight off his shoulders. He felt there was hope, and that something good should come out of the motivation Brandon had injected in him. He decided to while the hour Brandon had asked him to wait before contacting Mr. Takang at Cam Bank chatting with Simon, the owner of the telephone booth from which he had just called Brandon. He had thought of opening one of such booths for himself since it sounded like a new business that was gaining roots in town. He spent time talking with Simon about the business and what it took to start one of those. By the time he walked out of the kiosk, he was resolved he would start one of those as soon as he could talk it over with Brandon. His friend could lend him the money to begin with, and then he would repay him gradually; that was the only way to go without having to deal with high interest rates from other lenders. He smiled to himself as he walked on towards Cam Bank Bamenda situated midway along the main street in town—the Commercial Avenue. "All of a sudden, it looks as though things are slowly shaping up," thought Musang. "Praise be God!" he exclaimed as he walked on.

At the bank, Musang was shown to Mr. Takang, a smallish, skinny man with a rather strict expression in his bearing, who asked him, without even a smile, to sit down and wait for a second while he attended to a customer who came in before him. Musang was just sitting down on one of the chairs lining the wall across from a counter in front of Mr. Takang's desk but out of earshot of whatever conversation he might be having with his client when two young men about his age engaged in a very serious conversation of some sort sat right next to him.

"This country is strange *Massa*. Something this important and they write it only in French and do not even have it broadcast? How then do they expect potential Anglophone candidates to find out?" queried the skinny one.

"But for my friend in Yaounde, I would not have known. He said the announcement is posted at the *état-major*. The meaning is that if you go up to the provincial military headquarters here up-station, you are likely to find the same announcement posted on their notice board. The national headquarters cannot carry the news and the provincial will not." It was the thickset friend.

"But this is ridiculous, so if one does not have anything to do with the military camp how does one get such an important announcement which is supposed to be national?" queried Skinny.

"Are you going there to get the details or you are going to sit here fuming about how the government does things? Check on their notice board carefully. There is a week left to compile and submit the documents, which include a birth certificate, a certificate of non-conviction, a certificate of individuality, certified copies of your school certificates to show your highest level of education, a five thousand francs fiscal stamp, and I think ten thousand francs registration fee. If you can put that together and pass the *concour* (competitive exam), you may see yourself a military pilot within the next couple of years." Thickset stood up and walked out of the bank leaving Skinny behind. It was obvious he was waiting for the teller to pay him some money.

Musang had been listening but doing everything not to betray the fact. He immediately made up his mind to take a taxi to the military camp as soon as Mr. Takang could give him the money his friend had sent. Just then Mr. Takang, still looking stern, beckoned unto Musang from across the counter, and after looking at his identity card gave him an envelope. Musang looked inside and counted twenty brand new single thousand notes. Then he signed, on a sheet of paper Mr. Takang shoved in front of him, to show he had received the money.

"Thank you Sir."

Mr. Takang grunted in reply.

Musang stepped out of the bank feeling reinvigorated and transformed. It was as if he was noticing the sun outside for the first time. For months, he had barely touched a thousand francs, now here he was holding twenty thousand francs in brand new bank notes all belonging to him. He walked back to the phone booth with a sprint in his strides, and placed a call to Brandon.

"Hello-o! Hello!" It was Brandon.

"*L'homme,* Man I just want to let you know I have picked up what you sent. I can't thank you enough; I just can't thank you enough"

"Common now, what are friends for?"

"*L'homme,* you take everything lightly, but you don't know what this means to me, given how long it's been since last I touched money of any significant value. Thank you, and may the good Lord give you more."

"Now that's a better thank you, and consider that part of the amount we could have spent together had you not been busy trying to become a priest."

"Idiot! You fool!"

They both laughed heartily before Musang bade his friend good-bye and left the booth.

He could not believe that Brandon had sent him 20.000 francs. Musang smiled to himself when he thought of the money and how he had just heard of the competitive exam from those two inadvertent informants. From the City

Chemist Roundabout along the Commercial Avenue, Mankon's economic nerve centre, Musang boarded a taxi for the military camp up-station. Like all the township taxis, this was a yellow Mitsubishi Lancer car with the latest Makossa music booming inside. Musang was somewhat dazed as the houses sped past. He marvelled at the ostensibly carefree children playing soccer without cleats in front of some of these houses and navigating their way around sometimes dangerously displayed wares even as those producing the wares, and other professionals, went about their work seemingly without the slightest worry. Their disposition towards the chaotic scene seemed to communicate the fact that the environment, despite Musang's disapproval, was just perfect. The precariously displayed wares were indicative of the different trades practised inside the buildings and the surrounding vicinity. There were newly tailored shirts, trousers and different school uniforms hanging in front of tailoring workshops adjacent to another building in front of which recently completed upholstery chairs were displayed. Two buildings down the line, huge iron gates and other metal railings with dangerously sharp edges were leaning against the walls of a metal workshop like oversized spare parts for some beat-up vehicles parked nearby with mechanics in dusty outfits peering into their engines. As if this was not congestion enough, some bricklayers were pounding on moulds and producing cement blocks, which were immediately used in completing the decaying remains of an earlier attempt at erecting a house in an already crowded street corner.

"What a display of disorderliness charged with desperation?" thought Musang as he wondered about the role of the department of town planning as to him it was obvious there was no planning taking place whatsoever. Houses, trades, and their resultant wares or products, and human beings crowded the roadside in a manner suggestive of a certain spiritual chaos and lack of goodwill cannot amount to planning at all. Still haunted by how close the houses were to the existing roads, Musang wondered what the government would do in the future should the need arise and it decided to expand the roads. He wondered how anyone could feel safe with his veranda not up to forty feet away from a major road with a gushing flood of cars, which relent only to form equally dangerous traffic clusters with cars in speeding groups of threes and fours. He sighed and fidgeted in his pocket for money to pay off the taxi driver who had just pulled over next to the entrance into the military camp at Station.

When he stepped out of the taxi, he did not have to ask for directions; the location of the notice board was obvious from the number of young men surrounding it. Musang inched slowly towards the board, with his eyes already glued to the sheet of paper stapled to it. He let his feet do the job of searching for comfortable spots, between the stones, on their own. His eyes zeroed in on the announcement typed in black and made official with the logo of the armed forces stamped in red ink at the bottom of the page. The signature across the stamp was like that of adult learning to connect several lower case letters of the alphabet with a few upper case curvy lines. Indeed, it was the national communique announcing the upcoming competitive exam to take place there in the military camp. First, every potential candidate had to submit a folder with certified copies of the candidate's diplomas from the First School Leaving Certificate to the Highest Diploma in hand, the national identity card, a copy of the candidate's passport, birth certificate, a certificate of individuality, a marriage certificate for those who are married, and a vaccination card. There was only a week left before the deadline. After copying all the necessary information, Musang turned and walked out of the camp feeling tall: he had just received 20. 000 francs from his dear friend and then there was this competitive exam for which to prepare. If this was not a sign, then what was it? Where would he have taken all the money needed to compile what seemed to him a ridiculously conflicting and expensive list of unnecessary documents for this exam? He was as certain as he could ever be that he had to try his hand at the exam; it seemed to be his only choice out of his quandary if he could pass. They required one to be able to find one's way in French, and to be science inclined since the ultimate choice was becoming a military pilot or an aeronautics engineer.

It was a very happy Musang who stepped into his father's house that evening just as Ndzem was returning from church where a lavish wedding was being celebrated. After almost a whole month of not leaving his house for anything, Mojoko had convinced her husband to begin doing his work all over again, especially after the Bishop showed up in person to say how sorry he was that Musang had been sent away from the seminary, although there was hardly anything else he could do. She had reminded Ndzem that he was serving God not man, and that he must never forget that, else he would someday risk his salvation.

It took Musang four days to complete his dossier, which he submitted in the military camp up-station. Interestingly, the officer who collected his documents wished him well. "Do not forget to practice your running," one called out after him.

"I will not, thank you," answered Musang smiling in return.

It was already the third week since Musang returned from writing the final exam at Bafoussam, the neighbouring Francophone town in the West. The first exam was written in the military camp in Bamenda station where there were four hundred candidates vying for five positions; Musang was one of the five. He was encouraged to go on to Bafoussam for the final exam where two of the five would be selected and from then the government was to send them, along with those from other parts of the country, overseas for training. Some would emerge from training as pilots and others as aircraft mechanics, a choice they were to make depending on their performance in their exams. Those who perform best would have the chance to choose between becoming pilots or aircraft mechanics, whereas the rest would just have to fit into whatever slots would remain open when it got to their turn.

Musang had done everything without informing his parents. He was tired of breaking their hearts with fresh disappointments every now and then, so he decided he was just going to go through with this, and if all went well then he would inform them. However, if he did not make it in the exams, then nobody would feel disappointed or hurt since nobody knows anything about the exams. In any case, having gone through the first exam in Bamenda and made it to the final list, Musang knew that he would need the blessings and support of his parents and siblings eventually. As a result, on this fine day, just as the family was whiling time in the kitchen after dinner, he told them of his venture so far, and of the fact that he was expecting the final results that same evening during the 7:00 pm news.

Now, it was as if the family had an agenda for the evening even though they had planned nothing beside the routine habit of family members sitting by the fireside form time to time enjoying their after-dinner snack of roasted corn and boiled groundnuts. They normally sat like that munching and waiting for the evening news, after which there was a story-telling session. Finally, there was the signature tune for the news. The news went on for about five minutes before the newscasters got to the information about the competitive military exam Musang's family had only learned of that same evening. Musang was one of the two successful candidates from the North West. Everyone in the kitchen but for Ndzem, jumped up shouting for joy. They were clapping their hands in celebration as they spilled out into the yard with Mojoko leading the way. Ndzem, strangely calm and controlled, but glowing with excitement, turned and looked at his son with a smile. He stretched out his right hand and congratulated him. Mojoko, who had taken off in jubilation, was just returning to the kitchen with two of her neighbours she was particularly close to: Enjema and Ngum. Mojoko had already informed them of her son's success in this elite exam she and her family just learned about that same evening.

"He-e-e! Musang! So now you will be flying but in the air?" asked Ngum, one of the women.

Musang smiled without saying anything in return.

"Congratulations my son," it was Enjema, the slim, dark woman from the coast, married to Bambod, one of Ndzem's neighbours from across the street.

Musang took everything in with a smile.

"So when are you leaving?" asked Enjema genuinely happy for the young man.

"According to the announcement this evening, we have a week to report at the military barracks up Station."

"He-e-e! Mojoko, you hear your son?" Ngum called out. "He is now sounding like a soldier 'we have to report'." She traced a few dance steps in celebration.

About thirty minutes had gone by before Bambod showed up hurriedly at Ndzem's compound and joined the rest who had moved from the kitchen onto the veranda. He saluted Ndzem in the manner of a uniformed officer.

Ndzem smiled and answered back, "At ease! At ease!" imitating those ex-soldiers and police officers, like Bambod himself, who used to sit and tell stories of their days in the force.

"What good news is this? This child has made me to recall my days in Buea as a police corporal, with Sergeant Samson drilling us in readiness for parade. Bambod suddenly jumped to attention, ordered himself around as they would during a parade, marched from one end of the veranda to the other swinging his right arm. His left palm supporting the butt of an imaginary rifle, which was lying on his left shoulder. Bambod marched round the veranda twice, while treating Ndzem's position as the grandstand, before finally coming to halt in front of the women who clapped enthusiastically. Bambod always remembered his police days when he was happy, and he alone would drill himself to the admiration of all those around. When he finally sat down, it was to fill his glass with beer from a bottle of *Special*. He emptied the first cup with just a few gulps and filled his glass again which he set on the ground just under his seat. "Pa Catechist," he called Ndzem as he always did when something to celebrate came up.

"That's me," answered Ndzem.

"So the almighty God has finally heard your cry, and from now hence no more 'twenty-hungry' in this house."

"The Lord always rewards his faithful servants," Ndzem answered.

"Amen!" chorused the rest.

The neighbours kept trickling in until the many seats in Ndzem's parlour were all occupied. The crowd became rowdier as the night aged, with Ndzem sending for more drinks each time a new arrival showed up. The celebration went on late into the night.

The week before Musang was to report at the military camp in Station went by like a single breath. Early on the day of his departure, he stood up around 5:00am, had his bath, got dressed, and was sitting in the parlour waiting for his father; there was morning Mass at 6:00am and the family is always present. His mother was up by 4:00am and so the meal she was cooking was already done and she was taking her time dishing it as, from the kitchen, she monitored her husband's movements within. She could imagine him putting together all his regalia as successor to his grandfather, which included a traditional raffia bag, a *jumpa* and the big, black, drinking horn carved out of a buffalo's horn. On days like this, it was certain he would invoke the ancestors for his son's safety even before he went into church. "Az-a-h!" Mojoko called out to Musang's younger sister, "come and take this food to your father's table."

When Ndzem emerged from his room, he cleared his throat, a signal to alert the family that he was out of his room and ready. Mojoko half-walked and stooped out of the kitchen into the parlour where the family was now assembled: Ndzem, Musang, Ngu, Azah the only girl, and the last boy,

Mabémè, were already seated and full of expectations. Ndzem walked to his chair and sat down so heavily that both his feet bounced off the ground temporarily before landing back.

"Are you set?" he asked

Musang nodded in agreement.

"So some of you by choice will become pilots and others would learn how to repair the military planes that the pilots would be flying." Ndzem started as if the conversation had been going on forever; may be it had been going on in his head ever since the night before as he thought of Musang's impending departure. "When things like this happen, we must thank the ancestors and ask them to take care of their child as he travels." Ndzem stood up and asked Musang to stand up and come to him. He complied. "Take off your shoes." Musang did as instructed. Just then, Mojoko left the room and returned with a bowl of clean drinking water. Ndzem dipped his hand into the raffia bag hanging across from his right shoulder and pulled out the black buffalo horn used for drinking palm wine on very special occasions. He slapped the horn across his left palm thrice, blew into it before looking inside to check for any dirt. Satisfied that the horn was clean, he showed it to Mojoko who filled it with clean water.

Like the head of the family, Ndzem called on the ancestors of his family, the souls of his dead grandparents and parents as he prayed:

Wo-o-o-! Tabufor, Grandmother Atuakom!

Tata Tuilui-ntong, Nemoue Shom!

Here we are, gathered to send your child out

To a world we do not know where it is located,

All because of the blessings you all have heaped on him.

We call you all then to keep him company as he travels

Out, cleanse his face so that whoever looks upon it will

Fall in love with him and accept him as a friend.
Brighten his mien, open doors for him and let
No harm come his way. Who is that parent who feeds his or her
Child a scorpion? Then he or she is something else and
Not a parent. Who is that parent who laughs at a child in pain,
Then he or she is something else not a parent.
We will go to sleep and sleep soundly because we know
Musang is surrounded by you all.
Our Father, Yesso,
We call on you, bless this your child who is going out
To hunt; may he thrive, may his days be full of joy,
And after all is done, bring him back home like a true master.
We ask all this in the name of our Lord and Master Yesso,
Amin?

"Amen!" They all chorused after Ndzem.

As Ndzem was praying, he sprinkled some water from the horn onto Musang's exposed toes, tossed some outside as a way of keeping evil spirits at bay, and then some more within the house as he slammed the door shut, hemming in good spirits. Ndzem then took a sip from the horn before handing the rest to Musang whom he urged to drink. "Sit down then, let's eat." The family ate this early today because of Musang's impending departure. It was not really eating as such but just keeping Musang company as he ate. He was the one who needed to eat something, no matter how little, for nobody knew what his day would be like, and it is Ndzem's philosophy that nobody should leave his home with an empty stomach.

After their meal, Ndzem hugged his son and bade him goodbye since he himself had to rush to church to set the sacristy before the Reverend Father got there to celebrate Mass. "Call when you get to the white man's country. I hear calling from there is easier and cheaper than from here. So, we will expect you to do most of the calling. Let the good Lord escort you." Udzem spoke his last words as he walked out into the early morning darkness outside.

When Musang was done eating, he hugged his mother and siblings, picked up his bag and walked out of the house where Mojoko was still sniffing as she wept at the departure of her son. She did not know where he was going, nor did she know when he would be back. Musang walked past the church where he could still hear the voice of Father Alphonsus as he said his loud *"Dominus Vobiscum."* He smiled quietly to himself as he walked on imagining Father Alphonsus on the altar in his priestly regalia, his mind still harbouring thoughts of what it could have been like with him on that altar someday as a priest, imitating Father Alphonsus. He remembered his father saying that it would be a blessing to him if he could someday go to confession to his own son. He thought of all the advantages of becoming a priest and serving God directly instead of serving man. However, that was never to be; his bid for the priesthood had strangely turned into a catastrophe, which ended up teaching him a lot about human nature and so-called friends. His mind went to his dear friend Brandon. He would stop on the way, make a phone call to him, and acquaint him with his position. He may not have become a priest, but he would, by God's grace, return from training as a military Lieutenant and before long he would be climbing higher and higher, until someday he could become a colonel, Colonel Musang Ngang Tijie. Yes, that was his new goal in life, and he would get there by serving man who is made in the image of the Lord. He smiled to himself as he walked on picturing himself in full military attire.

It was to an awkward house that Ndzem returned; it was almost as if somebody had died in the family. Musang's space was obvious. It was his mother sweeping the front yard, a chore Musang attended to on a daily basis before taking out the goats and tethering them in a nearby bush for them to graze. Ndzem led the goats out, a little awkwardly but with pride, since his son had gone on to better things. On his mind, he replayed his discussion with Father Alphonsus that morning when he told him Musang had left for training to become a military pilot.

"What a waste," Father Alphonsus had lamented. "That was an obvious servant of God; he would have made a fine priest. I could see it in him, Ndzem. Musang was one of the few altar boys who knew exactly what it meant for him to be on the altar."

"That's true, Father. May God's will be done," answered Ndzem with so much conviction that even Father looked at him with a lot of admiration at the profundity of his faith which never seemed to fail him and his family, their travails and woes notwithstanding.

"That is true. May God's will be done with that fine young man."

Ndzem came out of his thoughts when he felt being watched. Indeed, Ambe his friend and neighbour was watching him. Ambe walked with a slight limp in the left leg, supported by a cane: the result of a serious motorcycle accident that left his friend who was giving him a ride, dead.

"Ndzem! Are you okay? What would your son say should he hear that he has barely left and his father is beginning to hold dialogues alone?"

"Ambe, you can only hold dialogues with somebody else; you mean a monologue."

"*Oh-ho*, now you have become grammar teacher when common doctrine is almost driving you crazy."

"What are you talking about in any case?" answered Ndzem laughing aloud.

"I am talking about you talking alone. Is everything okay? Or is your Bakweri woman threatening to leave you?"

"Ambe, who doesn't talk alone? Show me that man or woman with children who has never caught himself or herself talking alone."

"My brother, what would these children today not pass one through?"

"*Oh-ho*, there you go. As for my wife leaving me, don't mind Mojoko. Where would she leave me to at this age?" questioned Ndzem with pride.

"Begin to joke, or you have forgotten that you are married to a beautiful Bakweri woman. Have you forgotten it is said that if a Bakweri girl does not get married at least twice then she thinks she is not beautiful?"

"That is nonsense talk Ambe, utter nonsense! Whatever the case, show me the man that would dare to take Mojoko from me. That is the day they will know I am the son of late Pa Tijie. In any case, that your theory does not hold true to Bakweri women alone; if a man does not take good care of his woman, she is likely to leave."

"I am telling what they say about those coastal girls and you are talking nonsense."

"If you are in line waiting for Mojoko to leave me for you, then you will wait until dogs begin talking. Take your gun and go to the forest and hunt for your own Bakweri girl, don't come and stand by my door waiting for the day Mojoko would leave. What are you doing spying on me by the way?"

"Pa Catechist!" Ambe called out still laughing at Ndzem and his hunting idea.

"*Enhe!*"

"Spying on you?"

"Is that not what you were doing?"

"Look at this poor *Graffi* man trying to sound important. I was just making sure you were all right. You appeared lost in thoughts such that you did not even hear me greet you."

"My brother, you have to pardon me. You are very correct about my being lost in my thoughts. This thing that your son just left like this is troubling me." Ndzem was referring to Musang. It is a sign of closeness between friends when one is willing to acknowledge that the other can be a parent to his children. "He did not seem too enthusiastic."

"What are you talking about? Who in his right senses would let such an opportunity pass him by?"

"But that's the point; he might just be going for this thing because of the opportunity it presents and not because he is happy becoming a soldier or pilot or soldier-pilot, whatever you people call them."

"Pa Catechist, there are not that many who would turn down such an opportunity. If he turns it down, what is he trying to become then?"

"I hear you, but there are nobler and more gratifying professions and vocations out there although without all the glamour attached to the position of a military pilot."

"Like what?" questioned Ambe with a rather suspicious and unsettling look on his face. "Like what?" he reiterated with a knowing air about him. "As you have seen, Musang is not the man who does not know what he wants. Should this turn out to be something he does not like, he will let you know, although we pray he likes this given his age now. Time waits for nobody they say."

"That's true," Ndzem confirmed.

"So instead of worrying, pray for his success. Don't they say a lot can and has been achieved through prayers?"

"Well, I wish the young man well, and whatever he chooses to become, I know he would excel at it. I have a calabash of fresh palm wine, which Pa Naah just dropped off. You want to try a little?" asked Ndzem.

"Why not? What is left for us to do at this point in our lives?"

They walked off to Ndzem's house still chatting.

When Musang got to the military camp up at Station, after his call and dialogue with Brandon, he was right on time. He met the other young man from the North West who had also been successful in the exam also just arriving.

"Good morning," greeted Musang.

"Morning! You must be Tijie?"

"Yes, I'm Musang Ngang Tijie."

"Good to finally meet you. I'm Ntum."

Their conversation was brought to a sudden stop by a soldier who cried out in French: "Are you the two candidates from the *concour*?"

"Yes, we are," answered Ntum.

"Over here," the soldier snapped, "and follow me."

The soldier led the way to a nearby door, knocked, opened, went in and immediately stood at attention in the presence of a young man sitting behind a desk and signing some documents displayed in front of him. The nametag on his right breast read "Lieutenant Ibrahim Bouba." When Lieutenant Bouba, stood up and walked round his desk towards the group that had just entered his office, he was a short somewhat stout and proud looking fellow whose bearing made it obvious he knew he was an officer. He asked the soldier who had ushered in Musang and Ntum to relax, and then he went on to brief them on the nature of their lives as soon as they left Bamenda. At last, he congratulated them on their success, urged them to be disciplined and obedient if they wished to be successful in the profession. All the formalities done with, Lieutenant Bouba walked the duo out to the front of his office and handed them over to another lieutenant who was already sitting in one of those jeeps without doors. They both exchanged greetings and then Lieutenant Bouba made it clear that the young men were now his responsibility. Lieutenant Akono, who was behind the steering wheel, looked a lot more approachable than Bouba. He smiled at Musang and Ntum as he pointed Musang to the front seat next to him, Ntum to the rear, and they were on their way to Bafoussam. If Musang had any doubts that his life was changing, this was the final proof: he was already being treated like a soldier, and a potential military officer, else he would not be given a ride in this purely military means of transport reserved for officers only. In fact, in his mind, whenever Musang thought of a military jeep, he remembered Captain Mbu who was stationed in Buea in those days, the late sixties precisely, who used to drive around Buea in a military jeep with a gun dangling from his right hip. Captain Mbu was his portrait of a perfect soldier and here he was *en route* to becoming one. They were to join the candidates in Bafoussam and then they would be evacuated to the next destination, which was yet to be revealed to them. There they would be transformed into soldiers and from there overseas to train as pilots and aircraft mechanics. Musang smiled to himself as orders were being issued them in French; it was as if the English language he was used to speaking in Bamenda had suddenly died. Again he smiled to himself, grateful for his secondary and high school days when he had been forced to learn French, else, where would he be now.

At Bafoussam, without any formalities, the duo was led by a Sergeant Mokolo into a kind of zinc shed, which was part of the makeshift hangar facing a small runway, and ordered to strip to their underwears in the presence of several military doctors amongst whom were two women. Musang did not find this funny at all, but it was obvious they had no choice. The two of them were asked to stand side-by-side facing the front of the room, and then the doctors went from candidate to candidate checking their chests with stethoscopes, asking them to breathe in now, and then deeply, and out and so on. Satisfied at last, in spite of all the previous medical exams the candidates had to undergo even before writing the main competitive exam, the doctors directed them into another room with Sergeant Mokolo leading the way. The sole occupant was a no-nonsense looking military barber with frightening facial marks: long lines on both cheeks that started from somewhere between his eyes and his ears, curving down to the edge of his mouth. He called them up one after the other and did a poor job scraping the hair off their heads.

"Now you are true recruits," he told them with a strange satisfaction he alone relished even to the point of licking his lips.

Sergeant Mokolo led Musang and Ntum into another shed where they were issued uniforms and ordered to bathe and dress up under the supervision of another male sergeant who came across like an automation. He must have seen too many recruits to care about their feelings. From the threshold

140

of the makeshift bathroom, the sergeant only called out commands until they were all done bathing and each was standing with a pile of supplies in his hands: boots, uniforms, and temporary beddings. Sergeant Mokolo took over again. Before dismissing them, Sergeant Mokolo who had been supervising them all through their arrival at the Bafoussam *Brigade* told them they were to line up outside within thirty minutes. It was the beginning of their lives as soldiers, so it seemed to Musang. Everything was going to be orders, shouting, and running around to keep to time.

Joined by two other young men, the Bafoussam unit, the group lined up outside as earlier instructed. A young female captain appeared from within the shed. Her beauty, even with only the barest makeup, was striking. She walked in a way that sent her hips thrusting gently from side to side in her military skirt. She looked so young she could easily have been one of them, if not younger even, but from her right breast dangled the insignia of a medical officer; so she was not only a captain, she was also a medical doctor. There was the cry of "*Garde-à-vous!*" from a seasoned sergeant who was standing by and everyone within earshot immediately stood at attention; even the four did the best they could to stand at attention. Without acknowledging the salute, Captain Mey Asana walked up to the men, introduced herself as the commanding officer of the Bafoussam *Brigade*. She talked to them about their brief stay with her. They were to leave before dawn. She, in fact, advised them to get the best rest they could before they took off, for it may be their very last for the next several months when they are being transformed into soldiers. She wished them well.

It was 4:30 am when a bugle sounded in their ears. Sergeant Mokolo stormed into their tent shouting out orders;

he seemed angry to find them still sleeping when he got there. He gave them ten minutes to bathe, get dressed, and line up with their belongings next to the small office by the runway. Musang saw the plane's light on the runway as it taxied towards them. His heart was pounding; he had never been on a plane before. When the plane came to a complete halt about two hundred feet away from them, Sergeant Mokolo's voice ripped through the early morning air again as he shouted orders bringing the four to attention. He then ordered them to line up and march towards the plane, and one after the other, they got on board and strapped themselves as instructed. As if it was a dream, they were soon airborne, heading towards their next destination. In the ensuing silence, Musang bowed his head as if dozing and prayed for a safe trip and success in his impending endeavour.

Two days after arriving Yaounde where they met with eight others from different parts of the country belonging to their batch, Musang's group was given permission to go into town. He seized the opportunity to call his parents in Bamenda. Ndzem was jubilant to hear from his son. Musang informed him that it would be months before they could hear from him again, but that all was fine and he was about getting into a more intensive phase of his training. He begged for his parents' prayers before hanging up.

Chapter 7

Although Musang called his parents and his dear friend Brandon from time to time to acquaint them with his location and training, it was late in the second year after his departure from Bamenda that once more he found himself taking in the familiar sites of the last couple of kilometres before Mile 1, on the way into Bamenda. It is at Mile 1 that most people arriving Bamenda are convinced they have arrived at last because of a huge signpost by the side of the road on which is written "Mile 1," and "Welcome to Bamenda." First, Musang had to report at the military headquarters in Bamenda Station to let the military authorities know he was in town. From the road where he got off the taxi, Musang smiled as he took in the military headquarters where, two years before, he had shown up as a civilian trying to deposit his documents; today he was returning as a flight lieutenant. He came out of his reverie when the sentry came to a brisk attention as he approached the entrance into the confines of the military headquarters. He was yet to be used to these salutes, but they made it clear to Musang that he was now a different person.

Close to an hour had elapsed when Musang walked out of the camp; this time he acknowledged the sentry's salute as he walked past. Musang hailed a taxi and saw himself enjoying a smooth ride down the meandering main road leading into the valley town of Mankon, and before long found himself in the belly of the town as the taxi dropped off a couple of passengers in the Old Town neighbourhood before taking him to his father's compound at Big Mankon. It was a refreshing feeling to see and be in his native city again.

The house looked deserted when Musang got out of the taxi. He paid off the taxi driver, and then picked up his knapsack and swung his arms into the straps as if putting on a shirt such that the bag was comfortably lodged on his back. He then picked up two other heavily loaded lightweight military duffle bags from the ground, one in each hand, and just as he turned to face his father's compound, he saw his mother taking furtive steps to peek at the stranger as if to ascertain it was her son. It took her a second or two, but she recognized her son. She sent a joyous scream into the air that brought a few neighbours outdoors at once. Mojoko ran to Musang, embraced and held him tightly to her bosom for what felt like a whole minute, even though the embrace lasted just a few seconds. Ambe, his father's neighbour, was at home so he and his wife, Ngum, stepped out at once and joined in the melee as soon as they found out the reason behind all the noise.

From the doctrine classes situated next to the church, Ndzem heard the noise coming from his yard. Its perplexing nature threw him off balance: at one time he was sure people were screaming and crying, only for him to hear others screaming and laughing clearly. "What must be going on in my yard?" he wondered aloud, his mind already going back to his sickly brother, even though, months before, he had received news of his brother's slow but miraculous recovery. He looked at his watch; he still had about thirty minutes before the end of doctrine classes. He was sure this was extraordinary. He had never experienced anything like it before, so he decided to send the catechumens home before the usual hour. He quickly locked the classroom and rushed home walking and trotting alternatingly, as the undulating and somewhat stony landscape would permit, yet trying to hide his anxiety. From a distance, he could see the group that had already gathered at his home until there were people standing at the threshold. "What could be going on," wondered Ndzem just as Mojoko was crossing the space between his house and the kitchen singing and thanking God aloud in a celebratory manner. Convinced that whatever it was, it had to be good, otherwise Mojoko would not trace those dance steps, Ndzem slowed down and carried himself with some dignity, which the original panic had taken away. He could hear Mojoko's commands to a child: "Catch those two big cocks and kill them. Get somebody to call your father."

"I'm right here," answered Ndzem some paces behind his wife.

"Your son has come home, old man!"

"Which son are you talking about? You will make the neighbourhood to think a man like me has only one son," Ndzem joked.

When Musang heard his father's voice, he stood up and walked out to meet and greet him as a sign of respect. Ndzem saw his son in full military regalia with the rank of a lieutenant glittering on his shoulder. He ran forward, embraced Musang, and then immediately raised both his hands up towards the sky with his palms facing upward as a sign of gratitude to God almighty. Then he ululated for some seconds before entering the house where there was a small crowd already gathered. Both his hands were still in the air as he celebrated and thanked God. The women immediately intoned a song of thanksgiving, which they all started singing. Mojoko stood at the threshold and beckoned Ngum, Ambe's wife, to step out. "I like the way you're sitting there laughing like a guest. Your son has come, and instead of you coming and figuring out

145

what strangers will eat, you go and sit there talking and talking with them."

Ngum laughed and gave excuses for not being able to think right at that moment.

Enjema, who had been away at the market and was just returning, heard the news from her children and left straight to Ndzem's house. "Tell your father where I am when he returns." She joined Mojoko and Ngum just as both women were about going into the kitchen to begin cooking, and before long, they were all ready to celebrate with food and drinks. Mojoko herself cooked her son's favourite meal of boiled plantains and fried fish in tomato stew.

After eating, Musang's family and the neighbours put him on the spot with all kinds of questions about his military training and more about flying a plane. The entire group was in disbelief that Musang could now fly a plane just after two years. However, whatever doubts they had were gradually eliminated by the numerous pictures of Musang dressed like a fighter pilot with his white flight instructor sitting next to him on the ground, in—flight, and so on. The final mark of authenticity was the fact that in many of the pictures they could see the American flag in the background. The grunting sounds of fascination by the time each one had gone through most of the pictures established their convictions about Musang being a well-trained fighter pilot who had learned how to fly a plane in America. There were other pictures of Musang in military uniform hanging from ropes up in the air, with a huge bag and a gun on his back, struggling to crawl across a huge pool of water down below. He told them that the first six months, roughly, was spent transforming them into soldiers with very harsh training that took them to different destinations within the country from Yaounde through Ngaoundere, and back to Yaounde for their graduation ceremony from the Combined Military Academy (EMIA). Because his specialty is flying huge military aircrafts, Musang had already been posted to Douala; he knew he would spend all his working life in the northern part of the country had he chosen to fly fighter jets, the base where fighter pilots remain in heavy demand. He had been given three weeks off, so he decided to visit family after over two years. The guests permitted Musang to go to bed round about midnight since they all agreed he was supposed to be exhausted. As the night wore on, so did the guests from much further away take their leave one after the other until only those nearest to Ndzem's compound were left. They spent the rest of the night eating, drinking and cracking jokes until they started falling asleep in their chairs before they all decided to stop for the day.

For the two weeks that Musang spent at home with his parents, he was himself according to his parents' assessment. In other words, his strenuous training and his new position of power and authority had not changed him in any way. He did not put on any airs because he was now a pilot and military officer; on the contrary he helped in every way possible, from doing the laundry to doing the dishes and even back to sweeping the yard and tethering the goats like he used to do. He and his family were suddenly the envy of the neighbourhood: his parents for having been blessed with such a wonderful son, and Musang himself for being so humble and hardworking. Everyone seemed to agree that that stretch of his life shortly after he left the seminary taught him all about how challenging life could be, and it made him truly humble, not that he had been otherwise, no! He just seemed to have acquired a better understanding of the fact that life could be so much bliss at one moment and at the very next, a nightmare. In any case, he became, convinced of the role of the Almighty in the lives of those who trust in, and look up to Him. He smiled as he remembered what one of his favourite priests in the seminary used to tell them: "God works wonders in the lives of His people, but He likes to remain anonymous; the fool goes on to claim the victory while the wise renders thanksgiving to God instead."

Musang had two days left to be with his family before leaving town. He had planned to spend two weeks with his family and one down south with his dear friend Brandon, who did not yet know he was already back in Cameroon. The last time they had spoken was when Musang called from Arizona, USA, where he was perfecting his flying skills. Even then, he was not sure about when he would return to Cameroon, and so he had only given tentative dates. It turned out to be a beautiful day with both his parents at home even before it was 3:00pm, so they found themselves seated in the parlour and just talking about his training and time overseas. It was then Mojoko broached the topic that now interested them, his parents, the most, given his success and the wonderful future that seems to lie ahead of him.

"So my son, do not be angry with me for asking, because you know how a mother's heart works. Now that you are back and virtually settled, I know you would need some time to rest a little, but are you thinking of a partner yet?"

"You know, like I've always told you, if you get married early enough, the advantage is yours: you'd be able to raise your children while you are still strong and that's a good thing. You see what I mean?" Ndzem had a quizzical look on his face.

Musang giggled before speaking. "I get what you are saying, Father; however, I believe I am going to disappoint you here."

"Disappoint me? How? You don't want to get married?"

"No, no, Father, far from that. I want to get married, but I do not know what you will say if I should tell you that my choice for a wife has not changed even after all these years?"

"What? You mean you still want to marry that Bakweri girl? Her name—Etonde?"

"Yes, Father, and you must remember that it was her father who didn't welcome us not Etonde. In fact, I have heard that for all these years she has refused getting to know any man. It's said she says she would only get married the day she hears I have been ordained a priest."

"That's not possible," Ndzem observed. "You mean even after all these years?"

"That's what I have heard from Brandon, Father. Remember that my problems at the seminary all started because I met with her briefly, when I went for Father Tilman's burial, just to tell her I was sorry for all what I had heard she was going through because of me."

"And until now you mean you still like her?"

"I do, Father."

"Well, my son, one of the things I have always said in dealing with your mother and my in-laws is that there's no pride in the affairs of marriage. This is a lifelong commitment and must be taken seriously, so if this is the girl you think you sincerely love, then tell me when and I am ready to go to Victoria again and talk some sense into her father's head. There are many Bamenda girls married down there and many girls from the coast here, what does he think you are taking his daughter to come and do? Or else why is his dislike for the *Graffi* man so strong."

"In fact, Father, I plan to go to Victoria from here and from there to Douala. It is my intention that while I'm in Victoria, I'll try to see how possible it is for me to meet with Etonde. If she still feels the way I do, then you'll hear from me. But this time her father has to agree in front of me before I'll ask you to come down and see them. With the military now, I can't be certain about how my superiors will behave, so I am unable to guarantee that if something like a "knock-door" has to take place I'll be there."

"You don't have to be there. If it is true that after all these years that young lady is still there and still willing to be married to you, then just let us know and we'll take care of the rest."

"Thanks, Father."

"We give thanks to God almighty."

When Musang got to Victoria, it was, as always, like a second home to him. He loved Victoria and Buea, towns in which he grew up, so he was always happy to get into town by dawn and take in the town with relish as he assessed how it was changing. The taxi driver dropped him off at Half Mile and as he walked away quietly, he could hear the driver's comments to the rest of his passengers.

"Can you believe that that young man is a military lieutenant? And we would never have known until those police men before the Mungo Bridge along Tiko-Douala road asked everyone to show his or her identify. He did not mind sitting behind in the van with other passengers, whereas *sans gallons* (privates), would come to the park in their uniforms forcing us to reserve the front seat for them. Indeed, it is true

150

that people who really matter do not give any trouble. What do you people who know book say? Empty vessels make the loudest noise; *no be so*? How so true, how so true," whispered the driver still in awe of Musang's humility. "*Au revoir mon lieutenant*," the driver called out after Musang as if he had known him for a long time beyond just the six-hour drive they had been together. Musang half turned towards the bus and gave a brisk military salute with smile as he walked on with his knapsack dangling from across his shoulders. His duffle bag had been full of gifts for members of his family and his friend Brandon, so one was now completely empty, but the other held gifts for Brandon and Etonde.

"Taxi!" Musang called out and made an offer to be taken the extra distance to Man O' War Bay where his friend with whom he trained, Lieutenant Mbonge, had been posted. It was a short visit to his friend but very important to Musang because he needed to be certain the lieutenant was in town. He told his friend he would get back to him early the next day since he might need him to drive him somewhere, given that he had just a few more days to be back in Douala. Musang was unsure where Etonde would be and so should he need to driver to her, Lieutenant Mbonge should be the one driving him instead of him going around in a taxi and all dressed up in his uniform. That settled, he took a taxi and was on his way back to town.

Musang was negotiating the last curve on the path to emerge in front of Brandon's door when he started calling out: "*L'homme! L'homme!*"

Brandon heard the first time but was not sure since Musang had not told him the exact date when he would be getting into town. So it was after the second call that Brandon exclaimed "He-e-e-ey!" and ran out navigating his way through his friends who were seated all around to get to Musang who was just stepping onto his veranda by this time.

They clashed in an embrace with Brandon tearing up almost at the same time. He quickly dried his eyes before his friends were sure they had seen him in tears.

"*L'homme*! Why the tears, Man?" asked Musang smiling happily.

"No, Man. I'm very glad to see you, I'm very glad, especially with all what you've been through. Look at you now." He hugged his friend again before withdrawing and looking at him in the face as if to access if there has been any change. "So how are things, Man? You look really good; but for the low haircut and your well-trimmed moustache and beard, you are still very much the same."

"I am glad you never saw me during those years when you were sending me money in Bamenda."

"Ugh, Man! Forget about those days. What are brothers for? In every life, there are ups and downs. I like the facial hair," said Brandon examining Musang's face closely.

"You do?" asked Musang surprised. "I just let it grow about a week before I came into the country, slightly above three weeks today."

"One would think you have been wearing it for ever. I like the way it is neatly trimmed and kept very close to the skin; even someone who does not like facial hair will not mind this; it fits you well."

"Thank you. It is just for a brief time that I'm enjoying this change in my appearance."

"So tell me, tell me…" It suddenly occurred to Brandon that he had not introduced Musang to his guests who were completely at a loss seeing Brandon display so much excitement removed from his usually calm and quiet self.

There were three young women and two other young men, besides Brandon, who were completely transfixed in the middle of whatever they were doing. "I am sorry...but -"

"No, no, no! We understand," they declared in unison.

"This is my friend, but he is my brother guys. To tell you the truth, he is my brother and I have not seen him for quite a while now, about five years in all. He has just returned from the US where he was training as a military pilot and has stopped by to see me."

"Wow, that's great," said one of the young men.

"*L'homme,* these are some of my colleagues, but they are with BICIC, our rival bank. I invited them over because they are new in town. This is Ondoa, this is Essomba, both from Yaounde, and this is Giselle from Bangante, Octavie from Loum and Béatrice. Béatrice is from Buea, but she grew up all her life in Garoua with her father who is with the Air Base there, Colonel Mulema."

"Quite a group," Musang responded. "Nice meeting you all. Please do not let my presence disturb you. Thanks." He walked past them into the bedroom, set his knapsack in one corner where Brandon had set the other bag, before crashing on the bed.

"You must be very tired and hungry?" asked Brandon who had just followed him into the bedroom.

"I am, but I won't die right yet."

"My friends were just about leaving. Just take a shower, that will refresh you and then we would go out for you to eat something."

"*L'homme,* you mean that even after all these years you still haven't learned how to cook?"

"*L'homme*, do not complicate my life, Man," answered Brandon smiling. "So even if I cook, that's the kind of food you would want me to receive you with?"

"Why don't you try eating some of the crap we ate in training?" Musang was laughing.

"I can imagine; all the more reason why you should eat something prepared by a real woman who knows her way around the hearth. Wow! *L'homme*, welcome, Man." There was a lot of excitement in Brandon's voice. "Okay, take your shower then. As you can see, a lot of remodelling has been done to this house with an in-house toilet facility now attached to my bedroom, according me the privilege of not having to step out at night in order to use the toilet. My landlord wants to keep me at all cost since I always pay his rents on time, so I am now living like a young tycoon." He spoke as he stepped out.

By the time Musang was done dressing, Brandon had returned from seeing off his friends. "So *L'homme*, how are you, Man?"

"This is your brother as you can see. I survived training and I'm now in Douala where I have been posted."

"Fantastic news; in Douala, under an hour's drive from here. How did you pool that fast one? Look at that chap who just left, whose father I said is in Garoua, Béatrice, she says her father has done all to be transferred to Douala, even after twenty-two years in the air force, in vain."

"I can understand. The point is that her father is a fighter pilot, and as you know those planes are mostly in Garoua so he cannot be sent to Douala."

"So what did you do?"

"After training as a fighter pilot and doing very well, one was given the privilege of choice. I chose to fly bigger military

154

transport planes since I knew these are mostly in Douala. With that, they had no choice but to send me to Douala where the demand for such flyers is high. That notwithstanding, in case of an emergency, I may be called upon to fly certain missions as a fighter pilot. However, everything being normal, I will likely be in Douala forever. But from time to time I will go to Garoua for refresher courses which cannot take more than a month at the most"

"That was smart. You like the whole experience I hope?"

"It's been great, apart from all the orders one has to take from time to time. It's interesting *L'homme*, but it also has its challenges like everything else. The problem is civilians are never aware of the kind of stress that exists in the military because all they see is the beautiful uniform. In my case, I'm a pilot, so I don't have much to do on the ground; once I have my orders and I'm airborne, not too many people can fling orders at me, so it's pretty alright."

"Have you been to Bamenda?"

"Yes, I'm just arriving from Bamenda. In fact, I had to go there first because there are issues I wanted to trash out with my parents before moving on."

"And I'm sure that besides me, you are in Victoria to deal with one of the issues."

"You're right, *L'homme*. Is she still there?"

"She's there. I think she is beginning to reconcile herself to the fact that you are gone for good. It was a tough thing you passed me through, I mean hiding the fact that you have been out of the seminary for years now from Etonde. Although she never opened her mouth to ask about you, I always could see the question in her eyes. Things are beginning to change in any case. There is this young medical doctor from CUSS, the University Centre for Health

Sciences, working at the Provincial hospital who is bent on going out with her, but there is no indication she has given in yet; I would have known. He's been heard boasting in places after a couple of drinks that he would get Etonde." Brandon saw the question in Musang's eyes, "I can assure you nothing is between them yet, but he is good looking, unfortunately too arrogant for his own good, and that will certainly work against him. Everyone in town is complaining about how he treats patients as if they are dirt. Otherwise, he is great. He even has a beautiful car besides the hospital ambulance that he is always driving around as if it is his private vehicle."

"Else how would people know he is a doctor, a big man? This big man problem with our people. I don't know where this inadequacy is from that one finds amongst our people, even with the very educated ones," lamented Musang.

"You know, one would think with all the education, they are the ones who should lead the way by being humble and of great service to their compatriots, instead they just want to be adored because they went to school and are in positions of power in the civil service. Man, this doctor guy I'm talking about is threatening to walk on people's heads in this town."

Musang sighed and moved his head from side to side. "This country, you mean people are still messing around with government property and there is nothing anyone can do?"

"Who is anyone when it is the 'anyones' themselves who are abusing government property and even the rest of us ordinary citizens without any godfathers and all that nonsense? Man, let's discuss something more important. Until the day we get a leader who really loves this country, we are doomed."

"Can I see her? Is she still at the same house?"

"Yes she is. She went back to school though, and she has just earned her bachelor's degree in banking from the University of Lagos in Nigeria. She took a study leave and so whenever she was back on holidays she worked with us. Those were the difficult moments because she would question with her eyes, but I had to behave as if I was unaware of what she was doing. Being as smart as that girl is, she could tell the situation was still the same, or else I would have told her. Besides holidays, she just flew in and out of Lagos like a man going to his backyard. She says it's only an hour's flight, so there were days she came into town on Friday and left on Monday. That chap has inspired me, Man, so I am thinking of doing exactly what she has done. She has not only promised to get admissions for me but keeps insisting that things are not as complicated in Nigeria as they are here—once you are qualified you are given your admissions and if you work hard the professors give you your grades. She brought back some forms, which I filled, and she took copies of my documents along with her; we are just waiting to hear from the university now. If all goes well, which she is certain it will because of the quality of my grades in high school, then I'll begin this new school year. I have also been granted study leave in recognition of the number of years I have spent with the bank without incident."

"I think that's a wonderful opportunity, *L'homme*, and you should seize it because we're not growing any younger."

"Say that again. Minus age, look at where you all are; I am the only one still marking time with my 'A' level certificate."

"You must never look at things like that. How do you know God did not place you where you are to help some of us? How many of our friends have you helped to get out of this country? How many? And then look at me and all that

I've been through, what would my life have been like without you?"

"*L'homme*, you think everyone thinks like you? How many of those friends even think of me today like you do?"

"It does not matter; if it is only one person who remembers the good you did, is that not something? Remember the ten lepers our Lord cured? How many came back to thank Him?"

Brandon laughed at the analogy. "Your training did not flush the seminary out of you yet?"

"It cannot. You think six years in the seminary during which the gospel was literally burned into one's consciousness was a joke? No way!"

"Let's go." Brandon said standing up and opening the door. "Are you nervous?"

"I think I am a little because I don't know how she will react."

"I know she has always loved you in spite of how much you've hurt her. It might take a while for her to convince herself that it is true, but I also believe she understands everything that has happened and should be able to take you back."

"Let's hope so," answered Musang.

It was a short walk to the building where Etonde was renting a one-bedroom apartment. "Her house looks dark. Where could she have gone?" Brandon was just voicing his thoughts. At Etonde's veranda, they met a man who had just emerged from behind the house as if he went behind to confirm that indeed Etonde was not around.

"Hello," he greeted Musang and Brandon.

"Good evening," they answered back.

"Do you gentlemen live around here?" asked the stranger with so much airs.

"No," Brandon answered.

"Okay, I'm Doctor Essembe from the Provincial Hospital. I was just wondering because I came to see the young lady who lives here, but there seems to be nobody at home. Okay then, good night gentlemen," greeted Doctor Essembe as he walked away leaving the duo surprised that he knew Etonde's house. To Musang, that was indicative that there was something already going on between them else he would not have known her house.

"That is ridiculous," Brandon put in. "There are guys who research a girl's residence and then show up without having been invited. This is Cameroon and not America where the girls would scream "stalker" from what I have heard. Here, we are just human beings interested in human beings without any strange motives other than getting to be emotionally involved."

Musang just giggled and said nothing. He was already used to Brandon accusing him of everything he had against western cultures as if he was solely responsible for the way things were in the West, especially America where the people kill themselves and each other as if it is just for the fun of it, according to Brandon. "*L'homme*, I have asked you to leave me with those your interesting viewpoints. I am the one who went to America but you know more about America than I do."

"The radio, listen to the news soldier, listen to the news," Brandon teased him further.

"*L'homme*, now that Etonde is not here, how are we going to know where she is, especially with this other hunter so close?"

"Let's go next door to that building there. One of her neighbours there is always aware of what is happening to Etonde. I can guarantee you; Limunga will know where she is."

"Limunga, that's a beautiful name."

"Leave Limunga alone; you are here for Etonde."

Musang just giggled as his friend teased him further.

"Brandon knocked on Limunga's door and waited for an answer. There was none. He knocked again and heard someone shuffling along, and then the door was opened.

"Hey Billy, looking for Etonde?"

"Do you know where she is?"

"She told me she would spend the weekend at Sokolo. Her parents asked her to come over, a family ritual, she said."

"Thanks Limungs," Brandon hugged her good night.

"Do you just go around hugging women like that?" Musang teased him as they walked away.

"She is my friend for your information."

"I'm surprised she is just your friend."

"Ha-ha," Brandon laughed, following Musang's train of thought. "*L'homme*, your man is finished, Man. I no longer have time for all that. Bessem, my new girlfriend, is putting me in line, and ever since Maggie left me, I have not been myself again. As a reminder, I stopped *buzzing*. Occasionally I might take a beer but that's it. She meant well for me but I was too stupid to understand, instead I was beating her up when she tried stopping drunken me from getting worse."

"That's sad, but at least you benefitted something from her even if both of you did not end up married."

Not having met Etonde at home, it took over two hours for them to locate a good spot for Musang to eat the local dish he was dying to eat—*fufu* and *ero*. They were talking and walking back to Brandon's place, when all of a sudden Brandon noticed that Musang was preoccupied.

"Everything okay, *L'homme*?"

"All is well. I am just wondering what I need to do to see Etonde."

"I don't think it will be difficult. You remember where her father's house is at Sokolo, right?"

"Sure!"

"Ok-a-y! Whenever you want to, we would just take a taxi, go there, and ask for her. We are no longer children, *L'homme,* unless the father wants to get married to his own daughter or else he does not wish her well in life, which, I am convinced, is not the case. You are not surprised to hear that Etonde has gone there to visit?"

"I was surprised, but preoccupied to follow up. So how did she begin going to their compound again?"

"Yes, that was because Etonde's grandmother who virtually brought her up, and Etonde loves and respects her in a way comparable to no other member of the family, walked on foot from Bonjongo to come and see her granddaughter about your matter herself. Man, it was the talk of Victoria, with everyone giving his own version of the story. After her father treated your family the way he did, Etonde boycotted their family home. She would not go there even when it was her mother, whom she loves so much, who called for her. Her mother came to her and begged her to forget and come back to the family but she would not. Not even beloved family friends could prevail on her to forgive her father and visit, until people started wondering what the *Graffi* boy did to her. When her father ordered her to Sokolo, she went but would not open her mouth until she left. A father's pride is always there, Man, but Etonde's father shelved his and came to his daughter's house but she would not let him in. On another occasion, her father came with close family friends Etonde has a lot of respect for; she let them into her house but would not say a word beyond her greetings to the family friends. One of the family friends asked her father to return to Sokolo and leave him and his wife with Etonde. They promised that they would get back to him when they were done with her. They stayed back and pleaded with Etonde who, for the first time in a whole year, explained to them how much her father had hurt her. I happened to have been with her on that day."

"Aunty," she addressed Mrs. Musongo who was with her husband, "the shame I felt, the pain I experienced seeing the man I loved treated with such spite, I cannot describe to you. I do not know what my father has against Bamenda people, but he is not the only South Westerner alive and so I cannot understand why he would make this whole nonsense so personal. My fiancé's mother is a Bakweri woman from this same Victoria. She was present, speaking to Daddy in pure Bakweri; even her husband grew up here in Bonjongo and Sasse and speaks perfect Bakweri, only for my father to storm out of the house after insulting me in front of the man I love. He left me embarrassed and stranded with my guests who had come all the way from Bamenda to ask for my hand in marriage. My father was not against my getting married but against my getting married to a Bamenda man who treated me with so much love and affection I felt like a queen whenever he was around me. I had never dated before as my father had advised because, like he always said, and correctly too, if I were well educated so would be the man to whom I was likely to get married. We are both still young, true, yet this man was on his way to America but wanted to leave me, his wife, behind temporarily, but my father cheated me of my future, my life, for some stupid unfounded hatred between people one can consider historical, and to an extent cultural, siblings. Who knows what we would have been today as a couple, given all the opportunities we hear are in America."

"But my daughter," Mrs. Musongo pleaded, "you have to forgive, you must learn to forgive. You are a potential wife and mother still, in which capacities you will find yourself hurt by so many people, from your husband to your children through friends and relatives, yet you must forgive them."

"Aunty I understand you, but my father should have known better. I never disrespected Daddy in any way; even before my intendant and his family came, I informed daddy. If a suitor's tribe is so important to him, why did daddy not make sure about that before causing a family to leave all the way from Bamenda to Sokolo only to be treated like beggars, if not worse? Even as I talk to you, I am still shivering because somehow it brings back some of the shame, embarrassment, and hurt I went through on that day."

"Okay daughter, we have heard and will pray you find it in your heart to let go and so forgive your father so your family can be one again. Remember that forgiveness is divine, and the good Lord urges us to forgive. Since Daddy here has to go to work, we will leave, but we'll stay in touch."

"*L'homme*, I breathed a sigh of relief when the couple left. I could not say anything because I could see where she was coming from with the whole issue. But believe me or not, because I had heard her talk about her grandmother after whom they named her, *Mbamba* Etonde, in Bonjongo, I advised her sister, Ewune, to ask her parents to send word about the situation to her grandmother. I hear her father was jubilant and wondered how it could have escaped him all this while. I heard her father himself went to his mother to explain what had happened and begged her to help him remedy the situation. They said she cried for long to hear that her namesake had not talked to her father for a whole year, if not more. She walked from Bonjongo on foot one Saturday and got here even before Etonde could get out of bed. *L'homme*, this girl has gone through a lot because of you. When her grandmother got here, I heard she banged on her door for quite a while but Etonde would not answer. She screamed in Bakweri language that she would kill herself before calling out, 'Etonde, it's me your namesake, open the door.' *L'homme*, I heard upon hearing her beloved grandmother's voice, Etonde ran out of her room, opened the door and hugged her *Mbamba* crying and then supported and led her into the house while begging her *Mbamba* that she was sorry she did not know she was the one. Her neighbours say her grandmother cried out in Bakweri: 'Who toyed with my heart and I am left uninformed until now?' So, you can imagine the love they have for each other.

"From what I heard, her grandmother listened to her and apologized profusely on the part of her father and assured her that even if she wants to marry a man from another country entirely, nobody would stand in her way again. *Mbamba* Etonde pleaded with her granddaughter and then led her to Sokolo that same day to reconcile her to her father. We heard that *Mbamba* Etonde lamented that she had always heard Etonde had genetically acquired so many of her traits, but she never dreamed that Etonde had also acquired that terrible temper of hers. In fact, if I am not mistaken, this is one of those weekends that the family sits together again so as to prevent that kind of rift from ever recurring."

"*L'homme*, I will go there tomorrow."

"I think you should before we are too late with this doctor guy sniffing around the place."

"Let's go through Half-Mile let me make a call to Lieutenant Mbonge to come and escort me there tomorrow. I cannot wait until tomorrow to call him, as earlier planned. We would dress alike and see if she would be able to make me out right away."

"What are you talking about? Why would she not?"

"Because of my beard, the uniform, and because I plan on going there when it's almost dark."

"If she hesitates at all, it will only be like a hiccough before she identifies you. No matter what, a woman will always recognize her man at some point down the line, I believe."

"That's correct, and I think that's what I mean. I want to see how long it will take her to figure it out, and then her reaction when she finally does. That surprise is important to me, for which reason we will not be going with you because if she sees you she would naturally take a closer look at the men in uniform."

"That's true."

"*L'homme*, I cannot face Etonde when it is bright day, not yet.

"Just take it easy, Man. That chap is your chap so take easy; I know it is a little awkward after all these years, but she has not fought and waited this long to come and reject you now, Man, unless she is not well. Which is not the case. I think you're just nervous because you now know there is this other qualified guy after her and he means business. Even then, should both of you meet in front of her, just take control of the scene; she is yours, Man."

"Thanks for boosting my morale, Man."

165

"But it's the truth. And then, if all goes well, as I know it will, then I am going to be in big trouble with her too because she would want to know if I had known all this while and did not tell her. So when do I get to see you in uniform, Man?"

"Get out." Musang joked, yet he knew his friend was earnest about seeing him in uniform. "So where do you think I'll dress up? Please get me the iron so I can straighten my uniform."

Musang found it hard falling asleep that night. He could not believe he was in town with Etonde in that same town and he was yet to meet with her. Repeatedly, his mind replayed his experience with her even as he continued trying to figure out how Etonde would react upon seeing him, until he fell asleep.

Musang woke up to the whirring sound of the fan that kept the room somewhat fresh in spite of the humidity outside; it was hot. He looked at his watch at it was 9:00 am. He had been exhausted after the long trip from Bamenda to Victoria and so he had slept very well after all. There was still enough time for him to get ready and catch the 10:00 am Mass at Bota. On the way to church, Musang changed his mind and went to New Town instead. Etonde could easily go to Mass at Bota, being that she was at Sokolo, just a few miles away and with the Bota church being the closest to her family's residence.

It was exactly 4:00 pm when Lieutenant. Mbonge showed up as planned in a camouflaged military jeep. Musang was still dressing, so Brandon welcomed Lieutenant. Mbonge into the house.

"*Mon Lieutenant*, I will be with you in a second." Musang called out from within.

"Take your time; I already have a drink in my hand."

When Musang stepped out of the room into the parlour, Brandon was in awe, full of admiration for his friend in his sky blue military outfit, a tropical short sleeve suit with a deep sky blue beret. Brandon asked questions about all the different badges on the uniform until he was satisfied.

"Yes, that means I can jump out of planes with a parachute. Yes, that means I am a pilot; that means I am of the air force." Musang answered from question to question. "By the way *L'homme*, this is my very good friend with whom I trained, Lieutenant Mbonge. He will be flying helicopters all over Man O' War Bay where we have a military base. You people should get together from time to time, especially as he is new here. He is still single too. Who knows, you may help him find a wife. "

They all laughed as they walked out of the house to the jeep. Brandon bade them good-bye and retreated to the house while the two officers took off to Sokolo. After about twenty minutes, they were in sight of *Mola* Ngomba's compound from the road, although tall coconut trees made it hard to see everything around the compound. Musang became a little nervous when he saw people shuttling between the kitchen and the main building. It was a huge house with the kitchen behind and the Atlantic Ocean at the bottom of a low cliff about two hundred metres further off to the back of the kitchen. Etonde had told Musang how she loved walking along the shoreline behind her father's compound in the evenings. Now he was having a general idea of what the setting looks like although places were slowly getting dark. Last time the taxi had dropped his parents and him right in front of the building, but because the host family

167

was expecting them, it was difficult for him to look around as he was now doing.

The jeep zoomed to a halt to the left front side of the building such that people in the house could not see the vehicle, and anyone stepping out of the house would see only the driver side, the passenger side having been swallowed up by the huge shadow of a nearby tree with a thick bough. From within, everybody was concerned about the arrival of an unexpected vehicle right into the yard, and so there were faces staring out through the windows. Then Ekema and *Mola* Ngomba stepped out onto the veranda from where they looked on in anticipation without daring any further. Through a side window with a view through the internal kitchen and pantry area, Musang could see, in a bedroom, a figure he was convinced was Etonde talking to somebody since, with the approaching darkness, the house was already lighted. She did not seem to care about what was going on outside. Lieutenant Mbonge stepped out of the vehicle as agreed upon and approached Ekema and *Mola* Ngomba on the veranda.

"Good evening Sir," he greeted with confidence.

"Evening!" answered *Mola* Ngomba.

"I am sorry to come into your compound this late and unannounced, but I have just arrived Victoria and so I have no choice."

"That's okay; it's not exactly that late. It's just that this time of the year it gets dark a lot faster," answered *Mola* Ngomba.

"Thank you Sir. In fact, I am looking for a certain Miss Etonde Ngomba who works with Cam Bank. I went to her house and I was told by a neighbour that it is possible she is here at her parents'."

"And who are you?" asked *Mola* Ngomba stepping forward.

"My name is Lieutenant Esseme Mbonge, and I am new with the military here at Man O' War Bay."

"You are welcome, please step in," greeted *Mola* Ngomba. He led Lieutenant Mbonge into the house not noticing that there was another person in the jeep. The group of family members who had been attracted by the arrival of the jeep parted just beyond the threshold to let *Mola* Ngomba and Lieutenant Mbonge in, and then they all followed them into the sitting area of the parlour.

"Mother!" *Mola* Ngomba called out to Etonde who alone had stayed in the bedroom with her grandmother, *Mbamba* Etonde, even as everyone else stepped out to check out who it was that had arrived. "You have a guest."

"Mother!" *Mola* Ngomba called out again after waiting a few seconds without hearing any movements from the room where Etonde was with her grandmother. "Mother! I said you have a guest." He raised his voice more this time around.

"Me, Father?" Etonde asked stepping out of the bedroom supporting *Mbamba* Etonde who walked in a bent-over fashion because of this new pain she was having in her lower back. Etonde stared across the parlour at Lieutenant Mbonge who immediately stood up upon her entry.

"Who is he?" *Mbamba* Etonde asked.

"I don't know him *Mbamba*," Etonde answered in Bakweri as she approached the lieutenant after settling her grandmother in a couch. "Good evening and welcome."

"Thanks. Like I told your father – I believe he is?"

"Yes, that's my father."

"I am Lieutenant Esseme Mbonge and I'm stationed at Man O' War Bay, new though."

"You are welcome. Please sit down."

"Thanks."

"Ngowo, please ask the lieutenant what we can give him to drink." It was Iya who, so far, had only been watching quietly.

"That's my mother," Etonde pointed out.

"Good evening Ma," greeted Lieutenant Mbonge, making to stand again.

"Good evening officer. Please sit down, sit down"

"Thanks Ma."

"*Uwei*! See how handsome the child is in his uniform," exclaimed *Mbamba* Etonde.

Everybody laughed aloud. *Mbamba* Etonde spoke in Bakweri language, convinced the lieutenant would not understand. From his name, she knew he was not Bakweri. The laughter left Lieutenant Mbonge a little confused as he looked from face to face.

"Please do not mind my grandmother."

"What? Is she making fun of me," asked Lieutenant Mbonge smiling.

"On the contrary, she thinks you are very handsome in your uniform."

"Well, thank her for me."

Although *Mbamba* Etonde understood English very well, she always preferred speaking Bakweri while behaving as if she did not understand English. Etonde told her in Bakweri what Lieutenant Mbonge had said.

"Thank him for me too," said *Mbamba* Etonde before adding, "How I wish this one is here to marry my *Mbõmbo*."

"*Uweii-i*! *Mba-mba-a-a*!" Etonde cried out.

"Don't I have the right to say how I feel?"

"Mother, would you let them converse then?" It was *Mola* Ngomba himself talking to his mother.

"Ngowo, come and walk me back to my room since the soldier has taken my Name." *Mbamba* Etonde never made a secret of the fact that Etonde, who is named after her, is her favourite granddaughter.

Etonde waited for Lieutenant Mbonge to take a sip before she asked, "So how can I help you?"

Lieutenant Mbonge took his time. He looked at Etonde, her beautiful eyes with extraordinarily long lashes, her beautiful curvy lips and that charming smile with the tiny gap between her upper incisors and understood at once, why Musang was going through all the trouble. After hesitating for a while, he stuttered something: "I am sorry, but you are exactly all what I have heard you are and more even, so much so that I am already comfortable, drinking, and enjoying myself. I have even forgotten I am only a messenger. In any case, I am also trying to be careful so as not to make a mistake in the way I present the message I am bearing."

Etonde smiled again baring those charming white teeth and traces of a dimple on either cheek. She has a way of smiling and baring her slim delicate looking neck as she tilts her head a little to the left. "What kind of message are you bearing officer such that you are worried you could make a mistake in delivering it?"

"It is a message of love?" Lieutenant Mbonge blurted out directly.

"Love?" Etonde was a little startled but smiled it off. "You must be joking right? We do not have any mutual acquaintances to the best of my knowledge, so how can you bear such a message?"

"All the more reason why I am the bearer since we were sure you would never know where it was coming from. Etonde, please let me call you by your first name, even though I cannot pronounce that name as beautifully as my dear friend does. Etonde, I am from someone who is madly in love and cares so much about you, but he is worried and unsure if you would even want to hear from him."

A dark shadow fell on her hitherto bright countenance as Etonde slowly raised and put her left hand to her heart exposing slim long fingers with well-kept nails—polish-free. The depression her hand caused on her shirt exposed the top of her well-shaped, plump, right breast. Her mind went to Doctor Essembe who has been bothering her of recent and refusing to take a "no" for an answer. "No, please, not again," she whispered. "I really don't know anyone who can be so madly in love with me as you put it."

"Yes, you do."

"No, I don't." Etonde was beginning to like this officer's disposition already. "Sincerely I don't. I know only one person in my entire life who really loved me but things did not turn out as we had hoped, and there is no way he can come back into my life now; there is no way." Tears welled in her eyes and rolled down her cheeks as she thought of Musang.

"I'm sorry, but -"

"No, no... it's not your fault, Lieutenant. It's me; it's me." She whispered as she dried her eyes with her handkerchief.

"Tell you the truth, I am really enjoying myself talking to you. Can I go on?"

Etonde pierced into his eyes with her gaze, which betrayed her determination to go along with Lieutenant

Mbonge. "Of course, you may," she answered. "I don't know who you are or exactly why you are here, so you may do as you please."

"Thanks for your generosity. So what was his name, if I may ask?"

Etonde looked at him a little confused.

"The name of this man you said loved you so much."

"Oh! Of what use is that to you, Lieutenant? There is absolutely no way that you can know him. He was the love of my life and ever since I lost him, you'll not believe this, but it's been so many years now, I've not been able to get into a relationship. It's for that reason I'm at a loss as to the message you're bearing and even the sender."

"Well, since I am myself enjoying very much the way you talk, let me put another question to you so we can continue this conversation."

Etonde smiled again.

"This man you loved so much, were he to come back into your life today what would you do?"

"Lieutenant, please leave me alone, okay? I hope you have not been sent here to torment me," Etonde was so gentle in her ways and so soft-spoken, Lieutenant Mbonge was indeed enjoying his time with her.

"How can any man enjoy tormenting you, Etonde? Such a man would have to be a monster. I promise that this would be my last question to you and I would leave you alone. This man that you loved so much and he loved you so much in return, should he come back into your life today what would you do?"

"Oh you! I don't even know you that well, yet how you make me talk and talk. I waited for him for years, but he never came back. Now as I talk to you, he is a priest somewhere in Bamenda I am convinced. I had to stop trying to reach him, so I could heal else I might have died; my heart was always heavy for him. I continue to miss him, but that is life. Are you satisfied now? Yes, if he should come back it would be like returning a part of me that had been amputated if that poor image can make you imagine how I feel for him even after everything I've been through because of him."

"Wow, what a woman you are, as intelligent as you are beautiful. Yes, I am satisfied and thank you for your time. You are in every way the woman I have heard you are."

"From whom, Lieutenant? Who knows me so well in this town?"

"By the way, if you don't mind, please call me Esseme; keep "Lieutenant" for formal situations, or when I am around soldiers. Yes, you are very well known, Etonde, and you are everything they say you are…. What a terrible friend I am?"

"What?"

"You know, I came with a colleague of mine and I forgot all about him in the jeep. Here am I drinking and enjoying your company. This is incredible. Please let's bring him in." Etonde stood up and walked Lieutenant Mbonge to the door.

"Is he leaving?" asked *Mbamba* Etonde from inside her room.

"No *Mbamba*, he said he left a friend in his jeep and he had forgotten all about him. He wants to bring him in."

"Another soldier?" asked *Mbamba* Etonde.

"Yes, another soldier *Mbamba*, I think?"

In the darkness outside, Etonde could not tell the one from the other but that she was in the company of two uniformed men, so even when Musang greeted in a muffled voice, she just answered back as a matter of fact and ushered them into the house. When she got to her seat, Etonde

174

turned to take a better look at the second soldier. She adjusted her head and focused her eyes on Musang's face to be sure she was seeing correctly, but she remained unconvinced. How could this be Musang in an air force uniform, and with all that facial hair? This was not her Musang, at least not the way she remembered him. Musang always had on a thin moustache, neatly trimmed in a curve from one end of his mouth over his upper lip to the other end, never a beard or a goatee. Even as Etonde struggled to strip Musang's face of the hair to see what she could come up with Musang still held a straight face and did not betray any signs of recognizing Etonde either. However, when she inched in closer by leaning forward while still in her seat, Musang's lips slowly parted, revealing his teeth as he smiled; total recognition struck home.

"Mother! Mothe-e-r!" Etonde screamed. "*Mbamba*-o-o-o! Please come." It was a voice nobody had heard before; it sounded like she was frightened, in pain, happy, and confused all at once.

Mola Ngomba emerged with a machete in his right hand. "What is it, what is it?" he asked breathlessly upon finding nothing strange.

"Come and see something, Father."

The two soldiers were still standing and smiling.

"What is it?" *Mola* Ngomba asked all tensed up, as he was unable to find anything that could have worked his daughter up so much. Etonde was now standing as if hiding behind her father.

Realizing that nobody was making him out, Musang took off his beret, before greeting *Mola* Ngomba. "Good evening Sir."

"Goo-goo-good evening," stuttered *Mola* Ngomba staring into Musang's face and trying to be sure his eyes were not deceiving him. "*Eei*! *Eei*! *Eei*! My in-law, is it you?"

"It's me Sir," answered Musang smiling. Just then, Ewune emerged from the room and seeing Musang, flung herself into his arms with tears almost immediately running down her cheeks. Had Musang not been a strong young man, he might have lost his balance. Iya, still fastening her loincloth about her waist, and with hurried strides, emerged from another room with *Mbamba* Etonde slouching behind her. She hugged Musang and hung onto him for a while before *Mbamba* Etonde, who had just found out that this was the man who wanted to marry her *mbõmbo,* could get to him.

"*Iyae-e-e-e*!" exclaimed Iya. "Please sit down, sit down; let me invite you gentlemen to sit down for the second time. Please get them drinks."

Ewune who loved Musang so much was already in the kitchen heating up whatever leftovers they had in the house. Etonde had not spoken a word since after she called out; she was now sitting by *Mbamba* Etonde with her grandmother's left hand in both of hers as she stared at Musang from across the room.

"Etonde, you will not greet Musang?" It was Iya.

"Take your time, *Mbõmbo,*" *Mbamba* Etonde cautioned, hugging Etonde and holding her against her body while rubbing her back with her palm. "I know and understand. She needs time to take in everything. Just leave her to herself."

The food was all set, and more drinks brought in, yet Musang kept looking at Etonde who had been silently weeping in her grandmother's arms. It was as if the pain of all those years had suddenly resurfaced from deep down within and was crushing and drowning her. She clung to her grandmother and was joined by Ewune who was just done setting food on the table. Ewune was herself in tears as she looked at Musang with so much affection in her eyes.

"In-law, eat! Please eat. We will all eat with you." It was Iya.

"Mom," Musang called out to Iya, "I know a lot has happened and there will be time for all that, but seeing me here again, I think says a lot. Thank you for the food, but I am all tensed up myself, a little confused, and worried even though I understand. That notwithstanding, ever since I came in, Etonde has only been weeping, and as I said, I understand. I have myself wept over and over, but I must at this point say, so that I know where I stand, I will only eat if Etonde will ask me to."

There was silence and a sudden tension in the air as everyone turned and looked at Etonde still in her grandmother's embrace. She sat still with her tears streaming down her cheeks; it was only for a few seconds but it felt like a whole day.

"*Mbõmbo*, go and take your man," urged *Mbamba* Etonde.

Etonde, with tears still streaming down her cheeks, stood up and walked over to Musang who stood up as she approached. She hugged and clung unto him. Musang pulled out his handkerchief and dried Etonde's eyes, while shaking his own head in short swift movements to hold back his own tears. He made a place for Etonde by him at table and together the whole family ate quietly. When they were done eating, Musang was formally introduced to *Mbamba* Etonde, who said she was very happy to see him because she had heard so much about him although she was thinking he was a priest already. There was laughter. Musang pointed out that the whole transition from priesthood to an air force pilot was a long story and would be shared with time. The most important thing they should know was that it all had to do with Etonde, and through it all Etonde had always been on his mind. He informed the family that he had been posted to Douala and he had shown up again because he has carried Etonde with him all through his life ever since they first met until now, and if it would please Etonde and the family, for the second time he had come to beg for Etonde's hand in marriage. He apologized for seeming to be in a rush, but he pointed out that it was because now, as a soldier, his life was no longer his; he now belonged to the government, which could decide almost anything for him any time.

When Musang stopped talking, everyone in the parlour turned and looked at *Mola* Ngomba, who struggled with his low chair for a while but finally got to his feet.

"My son," *Mola* Ngomba was referring to Musang as he adjusted the loincloth about his waist. "I don't know from where to start, but I have been a foolish man," he dried his eyes with the sleeve of his white shirt. "I wish I could take back the pain I have caused you both, your family included, but how can I after all these years? In spite of what I did to you and your family, you have still come back for my daughter who came this close to losing her life for you because of my foolishness. It is true that ever since you left, my family has not been the same; you carried away the joy in this family, which I have again seen and experienced today after so many years. What else can I say? I'm anxious to meet your parents again if they can forgive me. But for the time being, Mother!" he called out to Etonde because of how she shares the same name with his biological mother. "Please, come here; nobody knows tomorrow. If I am here when

178

every formality is met, God be praised, but who knows. Nobody prays for death, but should death take me before that day, let nobody doubt my position. My in-law, please come this way." *Mola* Ngomba positioned Musang such that he was facing Etonde before he spoke. "My daughter and my mother, this is the man you wanted to marry a long time ago. Even after all this while, even with all what you two have gone through, he has again come back for your hand in marriage. It is said that a person's thing will always return to that person. Do you still love this man and are willing to be his wife."

"Yes, Father," answered Etonde with her eyes on the ground.

"For years I have begged my daughter's forgiveness for my stupid mistake. Son, I beg for yours too today before my own family, for I now know the pain I caused you two and both families for no reason whatsoever. We are all God's children and must not let our fears and shallow ideas and convictions cheat us of happiness that ought to be ours."

"It is okay Sir," said Musang as he looked in disbelief at the tears coursing down Pa Ngomba's cheeks.

"I am very sorry for hurting you and your family the way I did; thank you, and here is your wife. I know I speak for this family."

Everyone answered in the affirmative, and there was ululating and clapping, as Etonde was swallowed in an embrace by Musang even as Pa Ngomba walked back into his room followed by his jubilant wife.

A whole hour went by before Musang asked for permission to leave. His friend had to get back to base before it was too late.

"*Mbõmbo!*" *Mbamba* Etonde called out to Etonde, "Your man is ready to leave."

Etonde's strides were heard. She had bathed and changed into a beautiful purple gown that showed her curves, especially as she stood on those high heels. It was obvious she was going with Musang. Musang took her hand and they walked out into the darkness even as the entire family followed slowly all the way to the jeep. Musang turned and hugged everyone and with a promise to be back the next day. Ewune clung to him forever with her own tears flowing. "It's okay, it's okay," Musang assured her, "and thank you for everything." Musang then sat in front after helping Etonde into the rear of the jeep. After the goodbyes, Lieutenant Mbonge started the engine and they took off slowly until they got onto the tarmac, and then he gathered some speed. It was already 9:00pm. He dropped them off at Brandon's place and promised to see them the next day as he zoomed off immediately.

"Ewune really missed you; we all did, but for some reason, she was particularly attached to you."

"I know," Musang whispered as he walked on with Etonde's hand in his. "May be she understood before everyone else what was between us."

When through his window Brandon saw Etonde and Musang approaching hand in hand, he ran out and hugged Etonde; they held onto each other tightly, rocking from side to side for what seemed like forever. They walked into the house still clinging to each other with Musang following behind. Brandon brought out some drinks and they sat drinking, sporadically revisiting the road they have been on.

After about an hour, Etonde spoke up "I am feeling tired."

"Sure, it's been a long day for you, I can imagine," said Brandon. "Just a second let me grab this man's bags."

They walked the short distance to Etonde's place with Brandon carrying Musang's bags while Musang held Etonde's hand. Brandon bid them goodbye at the threshold, hugged Etonde, and then turned and walked away promising to come for lunch the next day. Etonde went into her bedroom, and after a while, came back into the sitting room dressed in a beautiful transparent, red nightgown that revealed her figure underneath especially when she walked at a certain angle in front of the light from the bulbs.

"There is one of my loincloths on the bed for you, and there is everything else you need in the bathroom."

"Thanks," Musang answered as he walked into the bedroom.

After waiting for Musang in the parlour in vain. Etonde went into the bedroom only to find him lying down facing the ceiling with the back of his head in his palms. He had bathed and had on her loincloth around his waist. She climbed into bed and put her head in the space between Musang's left arm and his hairy chest. His left hand came down on her body as he held her tightly to himself. Etonde turned, tipped her head back and looked into Musang's face.

"I am so sorry for all you have been through," he whispered.

"We, you mean?" she said with a faint smile. "It's alright."

"I'm sorry, Etonde, I'm so sorry." A tear rolled down his cheek and was crushed and smeared in between his and Etonde's cheek where her chin was wedged into Musang's jaw as she held back her head to look into his face. As she smeared further Musang's tears between both their jaws, by rubbing her jaw against his, her hands snaked round

181

Musang's body and she clasped him in an embrace. Musang was still trying to say something.

"Sh-sh-sh-sh-sh!" she hushed him. "Just hold me, just hold me; don't talk, don't talk," she urged, with her voice slowly dropping into a whisper. In the silence that followed, they could hear their hearts thumping against each other, along with the sounds of nocturnal insect screeching outside in the darkness oblivious of the minutes ticking by.

Printed in the United States
By Bookmasters